T.W.M. Ashford is a novelist residing in London, England. Amongst the damp and expensive gloom he can also be found getting far too excited about games and films, and, on occasion, appearing in monochrome.

His most recent work is the second book in the *Blackwater* series. Other titles include *Everything Ends*, *Checking Out* and his short story collection, *Mouth of Midnight*.

Books by T.W.M. Ashford

Everything Ends
Blackwater: Vol. One
Checking Out
Mouth of Midnight
Blackwater: Vol. Two

Get your free ebooks and start building your T.W.M. Ashford collection by subscribing to the mailing list at www.twmashford.com

EVERYTHING ENDS

(Or: Denouement)

T.W.M. ASHFORD

2

Cover design by T.W.M. Ashford.

Image: Tithi Luadthong/Shutterstock.com

Author portrait by Joseph Madden.

ISBN: 9781520764771

A massive and sincere thank you to all my
friends and family, and to anyone
who is kind enough to buy this book.

For Jo.

FOREWORD FROM THE AUTHOR

Hello, dear reader.

First of all: a massive thank you for picking up a copy of my debut novel, Everything Ends. It's a book that means a lot to me not only because it's the first piece of fiction I ever published, but because of *why* the book got written in the first place.

A good friend (and I believe my oldest, given that I'd known her for almost twenty years by the end - and at the age of twenty-four/ twenty-five that's quite some time) passed away a few years back. Much before her time, thanks to the absolute bastard that is Cancer. A little over a year afterwards, I began this book. About nine months later (just like a baby, eh!) it was released.

Be gentle with it. It's not conventional. It follows the various stages of grief that someone mourning the loss of a loved one goes through: denial, anger, bargaining, depression, and acceptance. It's driven more by its theme than it is by its story - not that it doesn't have a fun story too, of course. Imagery is everywhere, and I mean *everywhere*. You may spot things others don't. Maybe you'll spot things *I* didn't.

But a word of caution: by its very nature the story is bittersweet. Much like the process of mourning, you have to go through the bitter before you get to… well, nothing so nice as sweet, perhaps, but to reach the calm *after* the storm. At times it's raw, bleak and brutally honest. We *are* fleeting motes of dust on a rock destined to be engulfed by its own star. But that's not the end of the story, and of course, regardless of whatever belief one may or may not hold, we all know we're more than just that. We have love, and we have legacy.

If you're currently dealing with the loss of a loved one, or fear that such a tragedy might be looming over the horizon, then I advise that you park this book for the time being and revisit it when you're in a better place.

Otherwise, I hope you enjoy reading my fairytale for adults as much as I enjoyed writing it! It's an odd one, but certainly not without its charm. Just remember: the Pale One watches from out of the black.

The best of wishes,

Tom

CONTENTS

CHAPTER ONE

Laughter pierced the cloudless sky, shrill yet as warm and reassuring as the summer sun. The day was even more pleasant than usual, and the moment their lunch bell had chimed Harrington Primary School's swarm of children had taken to the playground in a religious fever.

The school had two areas available for break time. The playground was an expanse of concrete that welcomed visitors and played host to both the jungle gym and, to nobody's excitement, the hopscotch chalking. Then there was the field: a glorious Valhalla, an elusive yet enormous garden of racing tracks and secret enclaves. Elusive because for two thirds of the school year it was strictly off limits, and that last third began on April 1. This day was March 31.

But the heat and fresh air quickly evaporated any longing for the field; the children raced around the playground like miniature tyrants, each fighting for lunchtime dominance. Little girls gathered in close-knit communes, nursing friendships as intimate as they were treacherous. Little boys ran around after one another, playing the same game of a thousand names – Tag, Jailbreak, British Bulldog. Sometimes a boy would affectionately kick a girl before running away. Sometimes a ball would be booted beyond the school gates, and some brave adventurer would have to risk all, or at least detention, to retrieve it. Such is the way of the world.

Two children sat apart from everyone else, however. They didn't climb on the jungle gym. They didn't run around tapping each other's shoulders in a vain attempt to win games based on whatever rules had been whimsied that morning. They didn't move from the steps outside of their classroom. They enjoyed the sun as it beat down upon them, and they talked.

They were a boy and a girl, both the same grand age of ten. Well, the boy would always remind the girl that he was a whole three months and six days older than she was, parading that fact as if it was worthy of trumpet fanfares and standing ovations, but not a week's difference could be seen between them. His name was Vincent, hers Lily.

Lily had something wrong with her lungs. The veins got blocked, or something. She'd explained it to him once, but all the fancy words were lost on Vincent. He understood that Lily couldn't tire herself out like the other children in his class – she never took part in P.E., she never did anything that might break a sweat, let alone leave her coughing and wheezing. Anything more complicated than that and Vincent dumped it into the trash folder of 'adult stuff', the things only parents need concern themselves with. He just knew he enjoyed hanging out with Lily. She was nice.

So when the other boys came up and asked Vincent if he'd like to join the ranks in their game of Jailbreak (or Cops and Robbers, It, etc.) – and they still did, even as the months turned to years – he'd politely turn them away in favour of his friend. His best friend. Whoever had been sent to enlist him, most likely suffering in the throes of hay fever's snotty grip, would smile politely and disappear back into the throngs of madness.

It meant a lot to Lily. Sure she had girl friends, but none were as loyal or ever present as Vincent. It was a friendship that, if allowed to bloom, may have evolved into something greater.

They had met only two years or so before, but two years to a ten year old is an almighty slice of life. They'd been put into the same classes as each other but not spoken for the first couple of months, until they had to share a textbook one fateful math lesson. A mutual disdain of trigonometry and a love for a certain robot-warrior animation later, and they were inseparable.

And so here they were, spending a (near) summer's lunch together. His lunchbox housed a flat cheese and ham sandwich (with crusts, despite multiple protests to his mother), an apple (every Monday and Wednesday, for Tuesdays and Thursdays provided bananas and Fridays the special treat of grapes), a small carton of orange juice and a Mars Bar. Hers was a more five-star platter, sporting a ham and salami sandwich (no crusts - the result of a single protest), melon slices (her favourite fruit, and a regular staple for lunchtimes), a packet of salt and vinegar crisps (the crinkled kind, for they taste all the better), a bottle of blackcurrant juice and a bag of chocolate buttons. Rest assured; those buttons were shared out quite evenly between the two of them, each and every day.

The hot air plastered Vincent's blonde hair to his forehead. Mother kept threatening to cut it; it was long enough to flick him in the eye on occasion. He could feel sweat building up underneath his white school shirt, even with his blue, cotton jumper wrapped stylishly around his waist. But all of this was good. It meant that summer was finally crawling over spring's horizon. The air smelled hot and rich.

Fingers writhed in knotted coils. Moments hung in peaceful silence.

'Have you done the homework for Mr McCorvick yet?' came a voice as sweet as sherbet. Lily offered the bag of buttons to Vincent as she asked, and he dutifully clamped his fingers around four or five. They had melted in the sun, forming a blasphemous super-button. He devoured it in one.

'Nope, saving it for tonight,' he answered amidst chewing the chocolate. 'Was doing that Solar System poster last night, you know, for Science? Needed to catch up on English too. Gonna have to rush Maths this evening.'

He shrugged as if it would be a challenge. They both knew it wouldn't - Vincent had never been late to hand in homework in his life. Neither had Lily either, in fact.

Even if it were Maths.

They wolfed down the remaining chocolate and Vincent got up to stuff the empty packet into the nearby bin. It smelled foul and flies were hovering as if over rotten offal in the desert sun. He returned quickly, just as Lily closed the lid of her lunchbox over half a sandwich and an exhausted bottle of juice.

They leant back against the stone steps. Jet streams crisscrossed above, stitching together a blue canvas. They just hung there, with never a plane in sight. The two of them were adrift in a boat, the quiet amongst a sea of chaos.

'Coming to my birthday party?' asked Vincent. 'Three weeks away now.'

'Mmm dunno. Might have better things to do...' Lily teased.

'There'll be cake. And party bags.' He turned to look her in the eye. 'And at least nine balloons.'

'Well, I might turn up then,' she conceded. 'Maybe.'

They let the tide of silence wash over them once more, and drowned in the sun's comforting gaze. Time became immaterial. Vincent wished that he could spend eternity like this, soaking up rays and enjoying the simple act of just *existing*, and right then he could have believed it was possible. Anything was possible in that pure, timeless moment.

But then the bell rang and that was it; the moment was over. Nothing lasts forever. The jungle gym became an abandoned fortress, the playground a ghostly battlefield.

Children called quits on their games and lined up outside their classroom doors like dogs to a shepherd's whistle. Vincent and Lily got to their feet, dusted the grit from their clothes, and joined the back of their queue.

And so it will always be, or so Vincent thought. And with the infinite summer approaching he really did believe it would never end.

That was until the day Lily didn't turn up to school.

CHAPTER TWO

It's what they say - that there's sunshine after the storm. That's what they tell us. But I'm telling you; there is no silver lining, not to these clouds.

The car journey to the funeral was long, and quiet. Neighbourhoods passed behind the glass in an endless panoramic, each house lifeless and still. Families sat in their gardens, fathers mowed their lawns, but that reality was a far cry away. From inside the car the world was mere shades of grey.

Vincent's pupils fluttered as he looked past the scene, his eyes fixated on a point beyond. His head resting against the window, his mind was black; in pieces not at peace.

It was a Saturday and he should have been at home, watching his morning television. Playing a video game. Hanging out in the garden with Lily. Anything except going to her funeral.

'Are you sure you want to go?' Mother had asked. How can anyone be sure of something such as that? Nobody wants to attend a funeral. Nobody enjoys it. No, he wasn't sure he wanted to go. He didn't want to say goodbye; she wasn't gone. This whole thing was happening somewhere else, to someone else. But he knew he *had* to go, as if a ghostly hand was pulling him to the grave.

Mother had got his suit out of the wardrobe, a cute little three piece bought for him to wear at his Auntie Sarah's wedding four months or so ago. He knew he looked nice in it because both his Auntie and his (new) cousin April had said so, and they would have known because they looked lovely too. It was a really dark blue, like a winter evening's sky, and his mother found him a tie in cream.

But now, sitting in the back seat of her Fiat 500 as it navigated the last of the suburban labyrinth, he was pretty sure he didn't want to go. His stomach felt like a cavern, empty save for echoes and the chaotic fluttering of blinded moths. He'd tried to eat his scrambled eggs on toast that morning but, despite his mother's insistence that he eat something, he hadn't the appetite. Everything felt like cardboard in his mouth.

Sitting in the sun. Eating an ice cream. Riding his bike. Going to a funeral.

This wasn't *real*.

The world had stopped, and everybody outside were just actors filling the roles left in its wake. Fake smiles and wooden scripts and stage hands pulling all the ropes; Vincent was the only one watching from the stalls.

'You alright back there, sweet pea?' came a voice from the front, cutting through the silence. From the back seat Vincent could see Mother's curly, chestnut blonde hair spilling over her headrest, and her hand switching from gently caressing the wheel to changing gear with force. Her eyes, darker than her hair, watched from the rear view mirror. Her eyebrows were furrowed.

'Mmhmm,' replied Vincent, continuing to stare out the window.

'Do you want to talk about it, honey? We can still turn back, if you want.'

And how he did want to talk about it, how he wanted to open his mouth and just scream until all the jumbled thoughts in his head made sense, until they formed a coherent narrative on their own accord. All the words seemed to have coiled into a yarn of mellow violence, yearning to be spun into form.

But still he was silent, just shaking his head and maintaining that vacant stare. Watching the world go by. Watching the world spin to a halt.

* * *

The car crawled across the car park, little stones springing up and ricocheting off its underside. A miniature barrage of bullets later, and they had reached their destination.

The cool morning air crept under Vincent's clothes like a snake of ice, sending him to shivers. The sun was shining bright but today was no scorcher, no sir; it was as if the spirits had taken leave and spread out a ghostly picnic for visitors to walk through. Vincent pulled his sleeves tighter around his wrists, and hid them under his armpits. His mother didn't seem to notice, under her thick collared coat.

They must have been in good time, for other cars were joining them in regiment. Many of the faces that emerged from them were alien - blank, forgettable, devoid of expression. A couple Vincent thought he recognised from a birthday party at Lily's - the thought twisted in his gut - and one or two he knew from class. He knew he'd have to say hello later, but he wished he didn't. Every other person was just an obstacle in the emotional assault course of the day.

He and his mother crossed the gravel expanse, hand in hand. Normally he would have raced ahead, magnetically repulsed by such a public embarrassment, but today it didn't seem to matter. That, and it felt as if without her guidance he would never take another step forward. They passed under the iron archway of the graveyard's entrance, and the threshold was crossed. He could feel their presence, like fingers stroking the tips of his hair.

'There are so many,' he whispered, trying to fit all the gravestones into his sight at once. They were like the pebbles of the car park, and seemed to rival in number. A sea of faceless names and blank plots built from foundations of vibrant memory. Each and every slate had a story buried beneath, and some strange part of Vincent wanted to read the inscriptions on them all. It would take a lifetime, he was sure, but the impulse was there all the same.

'Yes,' replied his mother, her voice served with a drizzle of sorrow. 'Some of these go back even as far as a hundred years.'

A hundred years. Even Grandpa hadn't been that old when he'd died. Hell, he didn't think even Grandma was that old, and she was still weathering life like a mighty oak in a hurricane. He'd have to ask her when he next saw her. Maybe not when Mother was around though. She'd scold him for sure.

From the trees that lined their path came a rain of blossoms, spilling down in a pirouette of pink. How he longed for it to be the confetti at his Auntie's wedding again.

* * *

The box just lay there, nought but a casket of oak. Vincent refused to believe there was anything inside it but hollow air. She *couldn't* be inside. It wasn't possible. Lily was a constant, no more feasible to remove from the world than gravity. The only hint to her static body within that he could believe, was the small portrait sitting atop the coffin's lid. She looked happy, serene even, in stark contrast to the faces that now circled her smile.

Everyone had left the chapel, and the vicar was going through the last of his lines. All else was silent, save for the steady flow of sobs and a trickle of summer's breath through the leaves of trees.

He expected to feel sad. He expected to feel *distraught*. But all he had was this empty well in his stomach, a numb disbelief that sapped away at everything else. Where were the tears? So many others seemed swallowed by their loss yet here he was, as if only a visitor passing through. He was anything but, so where were the tears?

There was Pete towards the back, mostly hidden behind the rows of relatives. Vincent knew him from Religious Education class, but aside from a project together on the difference between Protestants and Catholics (apparently it mattered to the Irish) they'd barely spoken. He was with his father, whose expression was respectfully blank.

Emma and Hannah were standing beside each other, holding hands and bawling their eyes out. Made sense. They were best friends with Lily, the two that Lily spent all her time doing 'girly things' with. Usually Vincent felt jealousy towards them - whatever time she spent with them meant less with him - but now he just felt sympathy. Well, a hint of jealousy too - he longed to let everything out like they were. But he felt nothing.

He looked up. Even his mother was crying, albeit silently and with a certain grace and dignity. A trail the width of a single tear ran down from each eye.

Is something wrong with me?

He had expected Lily's family to be the worst of everyone, yet they seemed oddly composed. Preparation, Vincent assumed, to an extent. Her mother, Rachael, was worst, sobbing a steady rhythm into a hanky, whereas her father, David, was putting on a stoic face. A misery as great as his other, older child's (Reese, who was eleven) was fighting quite visibly to break through, however. Between the three of them they cast an image of a strong yet tragic family.

It was horrible seeing them like that. Not just because of the obvious tragedy of it all, but to see them picked up and placed into such a different context and emotional state to what had always been before: a warm welcome accompanied by wide arms and bright eyes. They seemed like another family altogether.

There were teary-eyed grandparents and even a newborn, who was somehow, against all odds, keeping everything together. Everybody else just fell into the crowd, a blanket of middle aged condolence.

But there was one who did not blend in with the others, who was not part of the mourning assembly. He watched from afar, beneath the shade of a great oak. He looked to be the groundskeeper, his overalls and tattersall shirt stained from dalliances with soil and grass. His face was old and gaunt, as if he himself had come close to death once or twice before, and he held his rake like a staff, its teeth cutting the air above his head. He watched in silence, with eyes that had seen this scene a thousand times.

The baby finally began to cry, and when Vincent looked back the man had gone.

The words came to an end and the coffin was lowered with patience. With the grace of an angel it descended into another world, until Vincent could barely see it over the soil. One by one the crowd stepped forward and threw white flowers onto the resting box, until they formed a quilt under which to slumber. Vincent felt his fall the furthest.

As the flowers themselves were blanketed with dirt his mother took Vincent over to Lily's family, transfixed by their daughter's gradual disappearance into the earth. They barely noticed them approaching.

'Oh hello, Anna. Hi Vincent. Thank you both for coming.' Lily's mother tried to smile but every choked syllable betrayed the emptiness lying behind. 'It means so much to all of us,' she added.

'Of course. Nothing in the world could have stopped us from coming. Isn't that right, Vincent?'

Vincent spun around, for he too had been mesmerised by the steady pattering of dirt atop wood. Bit by bit Lily was being erased from the present. 'Mmm,' he managed, before turning back to the grave.

How he felt that invisible hand once more; how he felt it pull him towards the plot. He wanted to climb in, tear open that bolted lid and see Lily alive and well once more. And she would embrace him, thank him for restoring reality, and everything would go back to how it should be. How it should always be. How it should have been.

'Let us know if there's anything we can do,' his mother said, hastily brushing aside her son's distraction. 'None of you should have to go through this alone.'

But this advice washed over the head of Vincent, who was watching his world close up one shovelful of dirt at a time. So transfixed was he, so hypnotised, that he failed to notice the groundsman standing beside him, the teeth of his rake hanging over his head.

CHAPTER THREE

The drive back was much quieter. Eerily quiet. Vincent didn't say a single word this time, not even when she tried talking to him. Urged him to talk. All he did was stare out of his window like a dog waiting for his master to return, his eyes like frosted hotel windows.

I suppose it's not completely unexpected, Anna thought, glancing at him through the rear-view mirror for the twentieth time. *Must be quite the horror for a ten year old.*

He'd be okay. It would take time, but her sweet little Vincent would be fine.

She wasn't so sure about herself, however. To see someone buried at such a similar age to her own child - it made her skin crawl. It wasn't how things were supposed to go. If there's a narrative playing out in this world, some sort of divine plan, then that's a paragraph that deserves a rewrite.

She only had Vincent left. She couldn't even imagine the darkness that would be left in his void.

They hadn't gone home after the funeral. She had taken him to Grandma's, who had been looking after Vincent a fair number of evenings as of late. She needed her alone time, and God knew she needed it tonight. Not that Vincent was likely to be much hassle; he'd got changed into a t-shirt and jeans in silence and kept that steady quiet right up until the moment she'd left. It was a little unnerving, but he needed alone time too. Sure, that's what it was. Digesting information; a process.

Give him a few days. He'll be okay.

One world ends, but the Earth keeps turning.

* * *

Vincent watched the cartoons cycle around, episode after episode. There was show about a cat that lived on the moon, or something, followed by the misadventures of a wise-cracking, green dinosaur. It seemed to have lost its picnic hamper to a gang of motorbike-riding sewer-crocodiles. He wasn't really paying attention. He was watching, but the pictures were just bouncing right off him.

Everybody has a Grandma. She's the type of relative that everyone can, well, relate to; a fountain of wisdom, a curator of concocted half-truths, a harbinger of knowledge reaching back to before Time was out of nappies. Vincent's probably knew the dinosaurs when they were 'yay high'. She was the sort of pensioner that could no doubt swing a mean handbag but never had reason to, for her wrinkled face suggested to any hooded youths that she could teach even Death a thing or to. Hard on the outside but soft on the in, she wasn't unlike an eclair.

She'd given Vincent free reign of the television for the evening, which would have been more generous an offer if she didn't usually give in to every one of his wishes anyway. Her titanium spine turned to butter when it came to her grandson. It was those blue eyes of his, so similar to her late husband's.

So here he was, lying across the width of the tasseled shawl that bathed the sofa, his head rested against one tiring hand, his eyes seeing another world. Noises just a distraction.

Cartoons were for babies anyway.

He seemed to be round Grandma's a lot recently. Mother had 'mummy things' to do - lord only knows what that meant. It seemed weird but things to do with adulthood tended to; it was best to just accept it and let it be. It meant more evenings at Grandma's anyway, and she always let him stay up late and helped him finish his homework quickly. She was smart, his Grandma.

He let his eyes go on a trip from the television to the rest of the living room. Each time he came over it seemed to take on a different shape; knick-knacks and ornaments moved like pieces on a chess board, squeezing their way amongst the shelves and tables in an ever-changing battle for supremacy. From painted clay dolls and foxes to wicker baskets and abstract arrangements, Grandma was both a crafter of art and an artist of craft. Youth fades, but passion burns bright until the end.

Vincent unstuck his shirt from his back. Man, was it hot. The morning had witnessed a breeze at least, but the evening air was still and dead.

Grandma had made one of his favourite meals - spaghetti and meatballs. It was delicious but Vincent had struggled with it. And now he was starting to regret the few forkfuls he'd managed to hold down; despite an overhead fan spinning round and around the room felt like an oven, and his dinner as if cooking for a second time.

The summer was like a friend of a friend - fun to be around when outside with other people but not so welcome when it was hammering on the door by itself, asking if he'd like to come out and play. And boy, was he not in the mood.

Not that Grandma seemed to be feeling the heat. *Maybe it's just me,* he wondered. She sure seemed comfortable enough, nesting in her wicker chair in the corner and piecing some feathered, knotted thing together. Perhaps her skin grew thinner with each blistering summer, and who knew how many of those Grandma had had.

Vincent's eyes went back to the ornaments, specifically the ones above the pretend fireplace. Nestled amongst them, the trinkets his personal guard, was Grandpa. Not literally Grandpa of course, that would have put a great deal of pressure on the mantlepiece, but a photograph from yesteryear, remembered in a simple, wooden frame. He smiled through large, thin-rimmed glasses that balanced above a thick, flowing moustache.

Grandpa had passed away about four years ago - it was difficult for a boy of ten to fathom exactly how long it had been - but he still held on to glimpses of memory, fragments of voice and image. Or perhaps he was marrying those vague memories to a fiction he had built up in his head, having filled in the blanks with photos such as these. He had been so very young then, after all. It was difficult to remember what was fact and what wasn't.

Grandpa hadn't been *that* old. Not walking-stick, incontinence pad, *who are you?* old, just a sort of wrinkled, experienced old. Older than Mother or even Grandma, but certainly not ancient. But things go wrong as soon as you stop bothering to count your age, it seems. Cogs need oiling and parts need replacing. And sometimes the engine stops working altogether. It was how things were supposed to be, in a way. It might be sad, but it was *natural*.

He wondered how sad Grandma must have been when it had happened. Devastated, he imagined. It was impossible to think of her as anything but this happy, jovial, eternal figure, but nobody gets through that without a tear or two.

A shiver ran down his spine. He almost welcomed it in the overbearing heat. Why did Mother need so much 'mummy time'? Was she hiding something from him? Was something wrong? Was Mother ill too? Suddenly his mind was full of questions that, before this morning, even his imagination wouldn't have dared dream up. Now they were real, and capable of bludgeoning force.

No. Cast those thoughts out. Mother was fine and this evening was no different from when he'd stayed at

Grandma's last week, or the week before. On any other day he would have been watching television, working through English homework, maybe playing one of Grandma's old card games that he had to pretend to understand.

But today was not like any other day.

Oh, plobnobbits. He was tired, and it was so, so hot.

He let his head sag onto the sofa. It was as if he was lying amongst the few rushes growing in a sparse desert, surrounded by leagues of dry sand and air. An endless burden of heat. He felt his eyes grow heavy and the rows of bric-a-bracs atop the fireplace flickered as if passing through an old-fashioned slideshow. By the time his mother came to pick him up at around ten o' clock, he was fast asleep.

* * *

Grandma watched Vincent from her chair, her hands knitting quite independently from her brain. Years of practice had left her grey matter free to ponder on the important things in life, the things with real *weight*. Her fingers didn't need to be micro-managed.

The boy was young. She loved him, she did; he was her favourite grandchild not just because he lived so close by but because he was such an ever present part of her life. It was like having a little boy of her own all over again. But he was still oh so young, and the young are so easily malleable in life's cruel hands. A death carries a great weight for all, but the fully-grown are capable of hardening their skin, spreading their shoulders and baring its brunt. The young can be crushed beneath it, flattened by its madness.

Vincent was being shaped by every pound of dawning reality that pressed upon him, and by every inch of innocence lost. *Little I could do*, Grandma thought, her hands threading stitch after stitch as if translating War and Peace into sign language, *without poking around inside that head of his. He's on his own, poor boy.*

Didn't have to be, of course. He could just talk it through. It wasn't as if everybody in the world hadn't had their own share of death to deal with. But he wouldn't. Not this little boy, not by the looks of it.

He can dive ever deeper or climb to the surface, the choice is entirely his. And only he alone can find his way out.

Click. Click. Click. The needles tapped together like the Grim Reaper's fingers against a reception desk, having rung the bell twice already.

She got up and folded the shawl over him. He was still, his eyelids sitting motionless in the cusp of early sleep.

Sleep tight, little one. That dark cloud hangs above us all.

CHAPTER FOUR

A thunderstorm had just passed. There was a charge to the air, a fleeting, spent energy that laced the very edges of his senses like sharp sugar round a cocktail glass. The soil smelled damp but the earth felt stiff underfoot. Sweet ozone sparked across his tongue, so he knew it to be true.

The cemetery stretched out before him, the thousands of white headstones standing like soldiers at attention. Each face was blank, expressionless, a tribute to the anonymous.

Vincent felt himself whimper, for no sound escaped his lips.

Night hung over graves like dusty drapes over furniture in an empty house, but the sky was devoid of stars. Without those tiny pinpricks in its canvas it hummed an electric purple, dripping a deep, dark light over the world. A hue that flowed thick as treacle.

Vincent spun around, his legs finally catching up with his brain. He was greeted by the cemetery's two enormous iron gates. They were closed. They were, despite Vincent's frantic attempts at rattling them open, locked. And despite the sun's departure the metal still burned to the touch.

Where the car park had normally stood was nothing but an empty void, a black placeholder for the rest of existence. A crematorium stood in the distance, cold and distant, its windows smoked and shuttered, as lifeless as its sleeping neighbours.

The blossom tree stood as still as an unwound clock, and no wind slipped through its petals.

Vincent began down the gravel path, though the world had muted his usual, heavy feet. Each step was like one through silent water. The graves passed by as if in an endless panoramic photograph - copy and paste scenery in monochrome.

He knew where he was going, even if his brain hadn't yet disclosed the details of what it was he looked for.

It was weird coming here without Mother. Cemeteries weren't inherently foreign to him - he couldn't count how many times he'd come to visit his father and grandfather - but that had always been during the daytime, usually late in the morning. And *always* with Mother or Grandma. Bathed in yellows and gold the graveyard was just a symbol; a place to remember, honour, or say goodbye. Under the cover of darkness it felt like trespassing on forbidden territory - that at the witching hour the garden of the dead would come alive.

The path crossed others, splitting graves into regiments like New York blocks. He twisted between their alleys like a rat in a maze, as if he'd made the journey countless times before.

And suddenly there it was, that rectangular hole in the earth, that empty space that Lily would call home for eternity. Her name stood out in bold across the pristine stone that towered behind; no date inscribed. The oak casket sat in its pit, still perfect and untouched by the mounds of dirt on either side. Its lid was shut with all the conviction of a crypt door.

She isn't gone, she can't be, thought Vincent, each syllable spelling itself out in front of his eyes before drifting into the rest of the mist. *There's nothing in there but lies and air.*

And yet he knew he had to see. He had to witness her inanimate body, the barren vessel the universe had left behind, for it to be true. And he knew it *wasn't* true; his heart denied it so. He would lift off the lid and the velvet cushions would be bare. Everything would be as it always was, how it would always be.

He stumbled into the grave, his shoes slipping through dirt that fell like miniature avalanches. The casket was cold, ice cold, and Vincent thought he could feel it tremble beneath his touch.

It was a lead weight on top of his fingers, but with them hooked under the lid he strained until his muscles screamed and his head pounded. He was a cable pulled to breaking point, a frayed rope ready to split. But millimetre by millimetre the lid relented, until one by one he slipped each finger inside the case and heaved it open. It swung with a heavy clang, threatening to snap back on its hinges.

His heart stopped, frozen mid-beat. There she was, eyes closed, as peaceful as if sleeping. Could he see her chest rise and fall with subtle breaths? Did those eyelids flutter with the wings of dreams? She was dressed in her favourite white petticoat and her hair was tucked behind her shoulders. She was serene, a perfect picturesque, same as she ever was.

Was that a ghost escaping from her lips?

He leant into the coffin, accompanied by a drop in temperature. The velvet felt like ice - glaciers cut smooth into ribbons. Inch by inch he drew closer to her, until his ear hovered a hair's breadth from her mouth.

'Vincent,' came a voice as soft as silk, as distant as echoes in an underpass.

She sat up as quickly as he pulled away, following in perfect parallel. Eyes blue as oceans stared into his own, tranquil seas that pulled him under. Her mouth curved into a smile spread through sorrow, and a spark of desperation fought through the onset of tears.

She pulled him against her in a fairytale embrace.

'Thank you,' she whispered, as clear as ice and just as cold.

She felt warm. There was life here; she was *alive*. It had all been a lie. A mistake. One horrible day, left to be forgotten by history to come.

'It's okay, Lily,' he said, pushing her away so that she sat at arm's length. 'It's all been a misunderstanding. They got it wrong. I can take you home...'

But where was home? Suddenly the sides of the grave seemed ever so high, and the dirt oh so brittle.

A darkness spread over the hole - not the darkness of the starless purple night but a true blackness, a pure void. It leaked like oil, drowning out the light.

Only the casket remained, the two children adrift in an endless sea of perfect dark. Waves of tar lapped against their raft. Yet still Vincent could see, as the last remnants of light shone across its surface, the blackness twist and writhe. Taller and taller it grew, a contorted pillar of shadow, until Vincent could see it was not just a shape but a man, a man with arms as thin as willow tree branches and a domed, eyeless face. And like a tree he stood there, his draping fingers cascading above Lily's head. Caging her body.

Dragging her into the depths below.

He leapt forward, almost plunging into the tar himself, and clasped his hand around hers. She was thrashing about as if drowning - *what do they say: remain calm in quicksand or else sink quicker?* - and already submerged from the waist down. That dark creature sank behind her, its talons hooked over the back of her head like a bear trap. Her eyes were that of a rabbit caught in one.

Her hand slipped loose but he caught her again, this time only by the tips of his fingers. Interlocked they strained, crushing their bones together. It sent rivers of agony up his arm, but still he hung over the edge of the casket. The oily black was up to her shoulders now, and still the figure pushed her down.

Then she let go. He felt her spill away like the ribbon of a balloon through his fingers; that moment it breaks free from your grip and you know that it's forever lost to the world above. The darkness crept up to her chin and over her ears. Her scream pierced the silence - a wavering, high-pitched screech that sustained long after the shadows had poured down her throat and she'd succumbed to the leagues beneath.

He desperately plunged his hand into the oily gloom, but under the surface there was nothing but deeper shadow. Further and further he stretched, and further and further the darkness crawled up his arms and over him, creeping over the casket until nothing could be seen but black, and still that scream screamed, grating like rusted iron and growing louder, and louder...

...

...until he realised that it was he who was screaming. He sat upright in the darkness, the surrounding shades of black growing familiar. He was in his bed, bathed not in purple night but the pale gaze of the moon as it peered through the folds of his curtains.

Just a nightmare, he told himself. *Just a bad dream.*

And for a moment, for just that disoriented second or two after waking, everything else was but a bad dream too.

But reality came swinging in just as did the shapes of his bedroom; here was his bed, covers creased and flung from half his body; there was his teddy bear, Martin - he knew he was too old for stuffed toys but it still felt wrong to confine him to the back of the wardrobe - lying in a particularly undignified position on the floor...

footsteps on the landing, here comes Mother to check in on me...

...and there were his clothes, neatly folded and left on the top of his desk chair. He must have fallen asleep at Grandma's; Mother must have put him to bed.

Punctual as clockwork, Mother threw open the door and flicked the light switch. Vincent shielded his eyes from the burning glare, and his room finally finished the transition from terrifying nightmare to boring reality.

'What's wrong?' Her voice came as sharp as the light. 'Is everything alright, sweet pea?' she added, her alert level dropping from 'Midnight Intruder' to somewhere between 'Relief' and 'Sleep-Deprived Resentment'.

Vincent nodded. 'Just a nightmare,' he said, feeling like such a child. He'd outgrown nightmares almost as much as he had Martin.

'Okay, Vincent. Go back to sleep, okay?' She hesitated at the doorframe. 'Want to keep the light on?'

A fragment of dream danced across the edge of Vincent's subconscious: oily darkness spreading over Lily's head and up his arms. He nodded again, and climbed back under the covers.

'Okay, darling. I'm just down the corridor if you need me.'

She shut the door as she left, leaving Vincent to snuggle himself against the pillow like a puppy in cotton wool. He was grateful for the light, for even though it burned red through his eyelids it kept him from falling back to sleep.

For he couldn't shake an image from his mind, a niggling suspicion that crept like spiders and wouldn't stop pulling on his curiosity. He couldn't have seen it; it was but shadows playing on his tired mind.

It must have been.

For what he thought he saw was that dark figure of blackness standing within the open frame of his wardrobe, staring with that blank face, its spindly arms stretched across the doorway and beckoning.

It must have been the shadows, playing on his tired mind.

CHAPTER FIVE

One nightmare was understandable, expected even. The boy had just lost his best friend after all. But when the nightmares repeated for another three nights, Anna knew something was wrong.

Well, wrong might be an unfair term. But something was certainly *worrying*, and if you asked her that was much the same. Of course he'd be upset. Of course he'd be different. Of course he'd display some unusual, even concerning behaviour. That, she was prepared for. What she couldn't accept was her little boy suffering each and every night. Nor could she stomach waking up to one more terrified, cracking scream.

Not to mention the breaking point to which she was quickly headed. She felt like a tired elevator cable, ready to snap.

He wouldn't even tell her what the nightmares were about. Still he kept quiet, a mute aside from the most distant, distracted murmurings. She'd get more conversation from a caveman she was sure, and about the same amount of grunting. Of course, she knew what it was about. It was about Lily in some way, bless her soul. The poor creature had had quite the effect on her little Vincent, and an even greater one now she'd gone. She just wished he'd *talk* to her about it. It wasn't as if she couldn't relate.

So after that fourth night, as she walked back to her bedroom with her bloodshot eyes retreating to the back of her skull, barely able to keep herself conscious, she decided to take him to the doctors.

And then Grandma had got involved.

It had seemed like a good idea at the time. Got a problem with the child? Speak to your own mother - she's been through it all before. But when she actually delivered her venerable advice, well, suddenly it didn't seem like such a good idea after all.

It wasn't even as if her advice was good! But somehow, through the unique sort of wisdom that all those bestowed with a thousand wrinkles seem to possess, Grandma had convinced her to give it one more night.

She was going to regret this, *that* she knew.

'It's all psychological, all up in his *head*,' Grandma had said, as if pulling the cloth from over some great secret. 'No point taking the poor lad to the doctors and making him think something's wrong with him. They'll just say the same thing or worse - give him pills.'

She had looked at Anna with the sort of judgemental eye that only the generation above can deliver.

'You don't want to fill him up with pills, do you?'

No. No she didn't. She didn't want to put him through counselling either. Her mother had a point. But she wasn't exactly providing a solution either, just dismissing them.

'What do you suggest I do instead then, if taking him to the doctors is such a waste of time?' asked Anna, in the tone of voice only someone of the generation below can employ.

Grandma had smiled and gone over to the wicker box in her living room, the one that doubled as a table. She removed a couple of ornaments and a used cup and saucer from its lid before rummaging inside, her fragile hands darting amongst what Anna could only describe as the result of a violent altercation between a ball of yarn and a small tree. After half a minute of complicated unravelling, and a series of deep mutterings from Grandma, a small object had been retrieved.

'This, this is a dreamcatcher.'

Anna managed to convey an entire conversation of disbelief in a single glare.

'Or dream snare,' continued Grandma. 'Or Ojibwe, in some cultures. The important thing is that it catches bad dreams before they reach the sleeper. Guarantees a restful night.'

Anna looked at the willow hoop, with its netted web hanging loose in the centre and eight tattered, purple feathers hanging from below. It looked like a bird had entered a spider's home uninvited, and left considerably worse for wear. It looked, to be honest, like something even a trader of homeopathy would think twice about stocking.

'Look, I appreciate all the arts and crafts, you know I do,' said Anna, trying very hard to keep the cap from bursting off her fizzing bottle of frustration. 'But I don't have time for your bloody superstitions! Do you honestly believe a magic wand is going to do the trick?'

Grandma tutted and rolled her eyes, knowing full well that such a combination would push Anna to the breaking point. 'Of course I don't believe in that mumbo-jumbo nonsense,' she replied, closing the lid of her table. 'I might be old, but I'm not senile. But it's what it represents that's important - what *effect* it has, not what it actually does. Vincent won't know if it works or not but he'll believe you. If he thinks he'll have sweet dreams, then his dreams will be sweet.

'It's all down to psychology,' she added, tapping her head twice with her finger.

Anna had to hand it to her; she had a point. Much like a placebo working even when the patient knows it to be so, Vincent would probably feel better for this 'dreamcatcher' even if he had doubts. She just hoped he *did* have doubts - she didn't want her little boy growing up sharing some of her mother's more 'interesting' traits.

Vincent was close to his Grandma. Perhaps he'd believe her at the very least. It was worth a try.

She took the dreamcatcher from her mother; it felt frail, as if holding it tight would cause it to unravel and slip away. It weighed next to nothing, a mere myth in her hand.

'Fine, I'll try it your way. But only for the one night,' she had added, and kissed her mother on the cheek. 'If he so much as gets tangled in his bedding tonight, I'm taking him straight to the doctors.'

* * *

So here she was, putting Vincent to bed. Preparing herself for another night of disrupted sleep and unsettling panic. Her head was starting to pound with the steadily accumulating hours of missed sleep.

This had better work.

She sat on the side of his bed as he pulled the covers up to his neck. He looked like a blind mole peeking its head up above ground; so tired and heavy were his eyes. He'd have no trouble falling asleep, it was staying that way that seemed to be the problem.

'So this,' she said, holding the frail knick-knack at arm's length as if it was roadkill, 'is a dreamcatcher. Do you know what one of these does?'

He shook his head, his right eyelid drooping like a drunk's. At least Martin the bear was giving her his undivided attention.

'Well,' she continued, 'Grandma gave it to me. And *she* says that it actually catches dreams before they reach you. All I have to do is hang it above your bed and hey presto: no more nightmares. How does that sound, aye?'

His eyes grew wide as she stood up from the bed. Suddenly he was paying attention.

'It catches all dreams?' He seemed torn between leaping from the bed like a terrier and becoming a recluse under the duvet. 'So I won't dream at all?'

'No, no, you will!' she said, rushing back to stroke his hair. 'Don't worry! See this netting?' She pointed at the loose, crisscrossing thread. 'It only catches the bad dreams. All the nice, pleasant dreams slip through the gaps and into your head!'

He studied it critically; if he'd worn reading spectacles, he would have been peering over the top of them with a single arched eyebrow.

'Grandma said all that?'

'Of course. And you know Grandma - if she says it works, it must do.'

Vincent smiled and rolled onto his side, his eyes shut tight.

'Okay. Night night, mum,' he said.

She kissed him on the forehead and stood back up. A small picture hung over the bed, and in it a ram rode a bicycle atop a mountain's peak. Absolute nonsense, but Vincent seemed to like it. She carefully lifted it from its hook, lowered it to the floor and put the dreamcatcher in its place with all the delicate precision of a surgeon.

Leaving the room she pulled the door almost shut - just enough of a gap for her arm to reach through and turn off the light. She watched her little boy, already swallowed by sleep, and prayed he was on the path to sweet dreams.

* * *

It was an hour to midnight when the curtains waved from the window. A sliver of moonlight stole into the room, but it did not steal alone.

A spectral element rode the nocturnal breeze, climbing up the vines that straddled the trellis against his wall. Its felt ran like rage, its echoes tasted of bee stings. It took on shapes from dimensions eyes couldn't reach. Every flutter of its wings was a scratch on the mirror of reality. It was the suppressed memory, the mortal fear, the deadly premonition.

It slipped through the gap between window and windowsill, brushing the curtain as it floated into the room. It hovered through the darkness, surfing through shadows like a paper airplane in the void.

The boy was still. His face was a blank canvas, detailing nothing. His bedding was sculpted into mountains and ravines, a barren landscape. Silence provided a soundtrack, overlaid only by the rustling of leaves outside and the steady *tick, tick, tick* of his clock.

Closer, closer. Such imagination, such fear to be siphoned. It came in to land, to absorb, to corrupt.

No. Something was wrong. The trajectory was warped, interfered with. *Tampered.* Instead of descending it found itself rising to the heavens - or, at least, the dizzying height of the headboard.

It kicked out with its phantom limbs, tearing at reality with claws and teeth that crept from other plains. But still it was drawn towards the dreamcatcher, a fly led to the web. Upon butchers' hooks it was speared, tied up amongst the thread. It struggled and struggled but it could not break free; it found itself trapped within dimensions three. It writhed like a snake nailed to the floor.

And beneath it lay the boy, a smile born across his lips.

* * *

For the three nights that followed Vincent slept like a brick. He didn't toss, he didn't turn, he didn't utter so much as a peep until dawn. The same went for Anna, much to her relief.

Well, what do you know, she thought. *Grandma was right after all.*

Who would have thought psychology could be so effective? She felt a little guilty about deceiving him, but then again what parent didn't give birth to the odd white lie or two for the benefit of their children? By the time he grew wise to the fact that hanging above his bed was nothing but a willow twig plastered with string and feathers, its use would be long over.

He wasn't back to normal - that would have been too much to hope for. The bags under his eyes were gone though, as were hers. He still picked at his gammon and eggs at dinner time and his lunch box came back from school largely untouched. He still kept to himself for the most part too, unwilling to talk about anything - school, television, games, let alone Lily. The only time she saw him smile was when she checked in on him whilst he was asleep. Who knew what dreams ran through that little head.

He didn't even seem miserable - *that* she could have dealt with. It was the numb, expressionless zombie sat before her that disturbed her the most. It was as if all emotion, all colour, had been drained from her boy.

Perhaps she would have to take him to the doctors after all.

Not that he wasn't improving in tiny ways. No, a mother could see these things. A few more vegetables eaten whilst his chips lay forgotten like the fallen pillars of Rome, the slight sparks of interest when something funny happened in a cartoon. He just needed time to get back to his old self. He'd bounce back; everybody does.

Don't they?

She wished she could see into that head of his, to read a transcript of his thoughts. To edit and correct; to fill in the blanks for him. Anna felt like a tortured spectator, watching from afar.

For Vincent, it was all like walking through a dream, apart from reality, a shadow passing through sunlight. He was waiting to wake up, to find himself awake in a world he could believe to be true.

At least he was sleeping better, and those nights provided a sweet release from the vacant days. For the three nights that followed he dreamt the brightest dreams.

But even the brightest light can be extinguished, and with the accident came the darkness.

CHAPTER SIX

'Get your shoes on, Vincent,' she called out, tapping her foot against the tiled floor. Fifteen minutes warning had been given, and still he was in the bathroom.

Anna looked at her watch. Just gone 11am on a Saturday. She hated wasting even a minute of her time and here Vincent was, lagging about like a ball and chain. Concrete boots, more like. It was as if he had all the time in the world. A slip of relief crossed her mind as she realised: yes, he did.

Two more minutes until five past the hour. Then she'd bring out the angry mum voice. Sometimes she wished there was somebody else in the house, somebody else in the family, to do it for her.

Vincent came stomping down the stairs like a buffalo down a mountainside, as if his socks were filled with lead. He flashed a smile of pearly white teeth as proof that he'd gone above and beyond the minimum brushing standards. It may have been artificial but at least there was humour lying behind it. She'd make do with any smile today.

She ruffled his hair as he bent down to put on his shoes. He'd moved on to laces – a bid to look 'grown up' in front of his classmates, it seemed to Anna – and was fumbling quite a bit, but he got there in the end. He stood up and nodded to his mother.

'Nice one, tiger,' she said, opening the door and holding it at arm's length above his head. 'Meet you at the car.'

He rushed out leaving Anna to lock the front door. It was a nice day, she reflected, as the sun beat down upon the back of her neck. *Perhaps we'll stop by the ice cream parlour on the way back*, she thought. *A little surprise*.

She walked the short length of the driveway, greeted by her son trying to open one of the car's rear doors. No matter how many times she gave him that knowing look, no matter how many times she told him that until her key was in the lock and the electronic *click* had signalled him to 'go' the door simply wouldn't open, he still tried the handle. He never learned.

'Sure you don't want to ride up in the front with me?' she asked, crossing over to the driver's side, keys in hand.

'No thanks,' he said, still hammering at the door's release. He'd never wanted to sit up front, no matter what the occasion. School run, birthday, good day, bad day; he refused to sit anywhere but the back left seat. Anna suspected that he believed the front passenger seat belonged to someone else.

She turned the key and the click acted like the gunshot at a race. Before her keys had even left the lock he was inside, pulling his door shut behind him.

Not sure what his rush is. He's not going to get far without me…

Today was the second Saturday of the month, and that meant one thing: *the Big Shop*. She got the essentials – fruit, vegetables, toilet roll, soap, the boring stuff – delivered each week (got to keep fresh, of course), but this was where the excitement lay. If by excitement she meant a time-consuming routine made only mildly enjoyable through the chance to spent time with her son.

She pulled out of the driveway, craning her neck as much to make sure Vincent was wearing his seatbelt as to ensure the road behind was clear. It was only ten minutes to the local supermarket, but you could never be too careful.

* * *

Oh, the aisles of vegetables, stretched out like row upon row of decapitated heads, looking up from the baskets of revolutions. Imagination proves a wonderful distraction for a young boy dragged around a supermarket.

The cool, artificial chill of the refrigerated rows wafted through the corridors of produce, doing mischief to Vincent's sinuses. It felt fake, detached, sterile. It felt like the cold of a morgue. He could imagine all the gammon steaks laid out on metal trays, white sheets pulled from over them by wiry men with a fascination with the morbid. Only, in his imagination, they wore waiter's uniforms.

Lily on a metal table, white sheet draped over her naked form, eyes closed for evermore.

Vincent shivered, and it wasn't just the pale air. It had been a week since the funeral and no, he didn't feel any better about it.

He didn't mind going shopping with Mother. It didn't exactly top his list of social affairs, but it almost guaranteed a packet of pig-shaped confectionery. Sometimes even a comic. *That* was the making of a good day.

But something was different today. Everything felt so *distant*. Blank faced drones pushing trolleys like worker bees, filling their caskets with the most mundane, unnecessary, trivial *things*. Everybody looked so dry and hung out, tiredly navigating the store as if on mine cart tracks. The canary pumping those trolley arms up and down, up and down.

It was as if the colour was running from the world, escaping through the cracks in the floor. Of course, that could have just been the harsh fluorescent lights.

* * *

They had wheeled the shopping trolley across the busy car park, its wheels spinning and flipping from side to side like a magpie in a tinsel factory. Anna had let Vincent push for a little part of the way, until drivers had started to weave through the spaces more erratically and Vincent had begun to veer the trolley towards the other parked vehicles. His license had been revoked, much to his disappointment.

It had been a large haul, made apparent both at the tills - *eighty-four pounds for the one week? seriously?* - and when lugging the bags into the back of the car. She was sure that the supermarket's bags were getting thinner by the day - a jar of bolognese sauce had become dangerously close to escaping and creating quite a suspicious mess on the floor.

Vincent sat in his usual back seat, flicking through the pages of his comic book. It hadn't taken much persuasion on his part to get both that *and* a packet of jelly snakes, but Anna had insisted he open them only after he'd eaten dinner. It was a pretty weak treaty.

Vincent, thumbing his way from page to page, had hoped his favourite cartoons would bring some sort of smile to his face, the way that they can creep up on you when you least expect them. But no smile came, and the pit in his stomach grew into an even greater void.

He stretched the seatbelt across himself as his mother got into the car, and put his comic down upon the middle seat. He got carsick every time he tried to read on the move and, even though it was only a short drive home, it wasn't worth feeling as if trapped inside a gyroscopic sauna.

Back to staring out that window, to watching the world flash by from his little pocket trapped in time.

Back to the silence.

The car's engine purred into life, his mother looking over her shoulder as she reversed out from the parking space. The car reminded Vincent of his old cat Jasper, fat and resting in the shade. It pulled out, lazily navigated the vehicular labyrinth and left the car park. The enormous beacon that made up the supermarket's logo drew away behind them, shrinking into a pale, blue dot.

There were no words exchanged, but both felt the weight of conversation hanging above them. He just couldn't bring himself to talk about it, to talk about *anything*. To speak would amount to admission of reality, and he had enough trouble arranging everything inside his own head let alone explain it to somebody else. It was a mess of tangled thoughts, and in the centre: Lily. He couldn't look past her face.

He glanced up at the rear view mirror, expecting to see his mother looking back, to see a smile push wrinkles around her eyes. To feel an ounce of warmth.

What he saw instead bathed his body in ice.

No eyes stared back, only the smooth, blank face of darkness from his dream. The same black presence that had dragged Lily into its depths. Its cavernous maw opened, spreading across row upon row of jagged canines like the greeting from a great white.

Vincent twisted his neck to look at the seat beside him, but there sat nothing but his discarded comic book. A cartoon dog was sporting a manic grin from the page, but else his row was empty.

'Something the matter, honey?' came his mother's voice from the front. Vincent looked back to the driver's seat, half expecting to see that nightmare fiend at the wheel.

'Just thought I saw something,' he replied, feeling the hairs on his arm relax. His back felt sticky with sweat. 'It's nothing really.'

But a question had risen from the deep, sitting on his lips like a siren on the rocks, ready to call out. He could feel it reaching - the unasked question. The box of unspoken truths, biding its time to be opened.

'Mum, why did Dad die?'

The car carried on down the road as before; his mother didn't slam on the brakes; she didn't jerk the wheel. There was no dramatic screeching of tires, no skidding to a stop. The world carried on as if those terrible words had never been uttered. The only reaction Vincent could make out was the slightest twitch under his mother's eye.

'Not now, Vincent, mummy's driving.'

Vincent looked to the seat beside his mother, the space that lay empty for the last piece of his family's puzzle. It seemed more bare now than ever.

'Was it his lungs too, like Lily? Or his heart? He can't have been *that* old.'

His mother's jaw stiffened, as did her hands upon the wheel. A very deliberate, hard silence echoed the one before. It was as if somebody had reached into the car, grabbed the mood and twisted its arm behind its back. It was a tense discomfort, one that was sure to build and build until it broke.

It hung for a few seconds before...

'Was it his lungs too, like-'

'Vincent! Why do you suddenly want to know? Why the sudden interest - why *now*?'

No sound but the steady rumble of wheels on tarmac.

'You barely speak to me for a week - a *whole week* for God's sake - and then the first words out of your mouth are about your father?' She shook her head before turning around to look at him. 'Seriously, Vincent?'

He hated it when she turned around when driving. It completely went against her usually careful character. He knew his life was always in her hands but when she turned around, just the one hand resting on the steering wheel, he knew his life was slipping from between her fingers. She only did it when she was mad; he felt himself wilt under those blazing eyes.

She turned back to check on the road. It was empty, a blank stretch of road save for a pair of traffic lights showing emerald. Either side was walled in by houses, the same design over and over again - each castle's garden protected by a white picket fence. Much to Vincent's relief she kept her head forward, instead channelling her gaze into the rear view mirror.

'I'm sorry, Vincent. I really am, I didn't mean to snap. I'm tired, and there's... there's been a lot on my mind. You know I don't like to speak about what happened and least of all while I'm driving...' She sighed. 'How about we talk about it when we get home, okay?' A light came on inside her head. 'Or how about we go get an ice cream, given how nice a day it is? And if you still want to talk about it, we can talk about it then.'

'But I want to talk about it *now*-'

'Well I *don't*, Vincent,' she shouted, her head twisting back around to look at him, 'and I am through having this conversation!' The car drifted ever so slowly to the right. 'That's it,' she added, sitting straight in her seat with the leaden finality of a judge's gavel. 'We're going straight home. No ice cream.'

'What? That's not fair! You can't promise me something and then take it away, that's not-'

'I promised you nothing. Life *isn't* fair. Now stop talking - I don't want to hear another word about it. Honestly, you say nothing for a week and then the only thing you want to talk about is that, *of all things*-'

'But mum, you *never* want to talk about it you always change the topic and I want to talk about it I *NEED* to talk about it *HOW DID DAD DIE? HOW*-'

Anna turned around sharply, staring deep into Vincent's eyes as his yell turned into a screech. She felt the hot rage rising like bile in her throat; she wanted to hit him but of course she wouldn't - never had and never would.

He screwed his eyes shut, head in between crossed arms, his voice rising higher and higher. She had never seen him like this before: a cola bottle shaken up, its lid slowly unwinding, ready to explode.

'Shut up, Vincent! Stop screaming, you're not a bloody baby! Jesus Christ, it's like you're-'

Her words were cut short, brought to a halt in a cacophony of twisting metal.

CHAPTER SEVEN

All I can see is endless white, an ocean devoid of blue, of life, of motion. There is no sky, no earth, no wind in the trees for there is no wind and there are no trees. Just an endless white, like a canvas that covers the Earth.

Where am I? What is this place? How did I get here?

I don't feel like I'm falling - surely I'd have that rushing sensation in my tummy like when I'm jumping out of a tree or riding a roller coaster. But neither do I feel ground beneath my feet; there doesn't seem to be a floor of any description at all. There doesn't seem to be a surface of any kind, just an infinite plain outside of any fathomable dimension.

I want to stand up, but I can't. I want to reach out, to stroke where there should be air, but I can't. I'm paralysed like a fly in a web, wondering from where the spider will stalk. I try to look down but there's nothing there; I'm but a disembodied thought - waiting, waiting, waiting.

Mummy, where are you?

Am I dead? Is this Limbo? Is this all there is: a sea of nothingness? Is the afterlife just some spiteful trick to numb the pain that reality's the best it gets? Well now I can feel panic, and that's sure as hell real. I want to go home, I want to go home.

Wait - how long have I been here? It doesn't feel as if much time has passed but maybe I'm thinking as slowly as an elephant, a tree, or the Earth itself. Maybe I'm thinking super-quick, each thought passing through my head in less than a millisecond. There's no sound let alone a clock to tick; this could be seconds, days, years. And just like that, another decade goes by.

That's if time even exists here, of course. Presumably not, if I'm dead. Dimensions one to three seem to be scarce, so why not the fourth too?

I have the most curious sensation, one of holding my breath underwater. It's not the pressure, nor the feeling of suffocation. That's the thing - there's nothing to breathe. It's the deprivation of senses - no sound, no taste, no smell. I'm not even sure I have sight, thanks to this wall of snow-blindness.

C'mon mum, where are you?

I should be awake by now. I should be awake. I know it. I can feel it. I should be awake.

Hmm. I was sure everything was a pure, retina-burning white before. Am I becoming adjusted to it like one would to the dimmest light in darkness, adapting to the flaws? It's just my imagination, surely. No, that white is certainly growing less pale, as if a shadow is thriving from behind. From behind everything. It's growing darker and darker, a journey from white to black.

I need to get out. There has to be a way out but I can't move I CAN'T MOVE. Please let me climb out, let me wake up, I need to wake up.

-this isn't real this isn't real this isn't real this-

Oh God it's halfway to pitch black now. It's like dusk in an old film. This isn't right, I should be awake by now, I should be back in my bed I shouldn't be here PLEASE let me wake up, what's happening to me? I'm trying so hard but everything is growing darker and I see no way out...

Mummy help me, help me. Throw me a buoy, lower me a ladder, anything I can grasp. I'm so helpless and all I can do is watch the shadows creep as the waters boil and flames lick below mummy help please help mum I'm alone and I'm scared and it's black now and I can't see I CAN'T SEE AND I'M SCARED AND I WANT TO GO HOME I NEED TO WAKE UP MUMMY HELP ME SOMEBODY HEL-

CHAPTER EIGHT

She sat beside the bed, hands pressed together over the bridge of her nose. It was all Anna could do to stifle the incoming breakdown, though silent tears still wormed their way through her clenched fingers.

It's my fault. This is all my fault.

She should have been focussing on the road. She should have kept looking forward. What was she thinking, looking back at him whilst driving? Was that what she considered *Responsible Parenting*? *Why not drive off a cliff while you're at it, Anna?*

I can't lose you too, Vincent. I couldn't bear to lose you too.

He lay in the hospital bed, as still as a cadaver. Only his chest rose and fell with the breath of the weak. His duvet covers were pulled up to his torso, his arms lay straight to either side. His hair - longer than Anna would like, she thought with a desperate triviality - spilled out across the pillow beneath his head like cracks in the pavement.

He looked peaceful, and if it wasn't for the sounds of medical equipment and rushing porters she could have believed he was asleep back home. But this was anything but a natural slumber.

She shuddered at a thought that kept freezing in her mind, shattering then reforming. What must have been his last conscious memory: a wall of steel death, crashing towards his wide, terrified eyes. She couldn't shake that fear, and as much as she wanted to reach out, hug him and calm that terror, those eyes stayed fixed on the nightmare approaching over her shoulder.

Eyes Forward. Always.

Her car had hit the Mercedes head on, crashing into its rear as it pulled out of its driveway. She didn't know who to blame. Herself, mostly. Though the other driver had been reversing without properly looking and, well, that was irresponsible too.

Of course, *they* didn't have a child in the backseat.

They'd collided at about twenty five miles per hour, not enough to total either car but plenty to cripple her Fiat's engine and seriously maul the Mercedes' rear bumper. Its tyre had been pretty savaged too - the axel might even have to be replaced. One thing was for sure; her insurance was going to be murder from here on out.

It was amazing that she hadn't been worse off. She had some light whiplash but had been kept from head butting the dashboard (or worse, flying through the windscreen) by her seatbelt. It still hurt to turn her head to the right - another reason not to turn around whilst driving, if there wasn't reason enough - but she'd been given a tentative all-clear from the doctor. It wasn't her own safety she cared about though, of course.

He'd been wearing a seatbelt, she was sure of it. She *always* checked if he was wearing it, and he always had been. He'd been wearing it when they pulled him from the car, like a rag-doll hanging from strings. But somehow he'd been thrown forwards far enough to hit his skull against the headrest of the seat in front - the *empty* seat in front - and knocked unconscious. He hadn't opened his eyes since.

The doctor had said his brain was healthy, that the scan had revealed no signs of lasting damage. And, aside from a nasty bruise on his forehead, he was physically well. Good news, Anna had thought, but there was something in Dr. Poll's words - a reluctance, a hesitation, a delicate treading across the unknown - that said the opposite.

He doesn't know what's wrong with my little boy.

Vincent had slipped into a coma and nobody, not Dr. Poll, not his colleagues, not fellows in other hospitals and fields, could offer an explanation why. The best hypothesis was that it was a defence mechanism to the impact, to rest and recover. Recover from what, nobody seemed to know. Poll had apologised, clutched his clipboard to his chest and backed from the room.

So here she was, sitting beside her little boy, beside her truest love, who lay as still as the dead. All that stopped her from breaking down completely was the assurance that, beneath the surface, her son was just the same as ever.

How long he'd be like this they couldn't say. Days, weeks, months? He could be trapped for years for all they knew, and every minute felt like a lifetime.

She overcame an urge to shake him awake.

Anna wasn't one of those people that hates hospitals. They didn't scare her; if anything, being surrounded by medical professionals filled her with the exact amount of healthy reassurance anyone level-headed would expect. The fact that nearly every person in every room was ill, broken or both was neither here nor there. It was a different story when her boy was lying within their walls, however. Now it seemed a prison, a laboratory, a death sentence. Everything was so sterile, so impersonal. Everything smelled of anti-bacterial soap.

Bland copy and paste furniture, featureless clones from Sweden, or something. Grey-brown blinds hanging in vertical strips from the windows. A plain, blue door leading to the toilet. A flatscreen TV against the wall. Some form of bastardised flower arrangement; cold metal in a plastic pot, twisted into 'natural' petal form.

She'd called Grandma as soon she could, of course. Who else would she call? She'd never thought of her mother as elderly until that moment, hearing her voice over the phone, distant and frail. Growing old; does that make oneself less afraid of death, or more? More, she suspected, at least when it regarded the deaths of others.

Grandma had said she'd be on the next bus to the hospital, but Anna had asked a favour of her. Grandma had gone to Anna's house first and picked up Vincent's pyjamas, a change of clothes - a little optimistic at this stage, she knew, but he'd be out one day - and some actual flowers for his room. Anna couldn't bear looking at that modern art monstrosity any longer. Grandma had turned up a couple of hours later, during which time Anna hadn't left Vincent's side, carrying a holdall that even a Peruvian cart donkey would balk at.

She'd offered to stay of course, dipping into the endless fountain of help all grandmothers possess, but Anna couldn't bear to leave Vincent's side. It wasn't just the fear of him turning for the worse, but her guilt that prevented her from leaving. Yes, she was tired and yes, she needed to rest, but she could do that here. She could do that by her little boy's side.

So Grandma had gotten back on the bus, and had called once home to let Anna know she was safe. And now Anna was alone, wishing she wasn't. She just watched her baby's chest rise and fall, rise and fall.

She glanced at the clock hanging above the bed. Almost four o'clock in the morning. No. Twenty-past eleven.

The plant impostor had since been replaced by the real deal, and Vincent's clothes lay folded atop a dresser adjacent to the bed. The holdall sat beside her chair, its zipper left open. There were still items left inside - assorted snapshots of Vincent's room.

A toothbrush, and toothpaste. *What's the deal with brushing teeth when somebody's in a coma? Will Vincent's teeth be okay unbrushed for weeks? If he doesn't eat then I suppose he doesn't need to guard against plaque. Oh, I don't know.*

A framed picture of Anna and Vincent at a theme park, riding a roller coaster. *Aw, that was sweet of Grandma. I'll put this next to his bed. Where was this even taken? Thrill City? World of Fun? Somewhere bloody awful, that's for sure. Vincent clearly loved it though.*

Martin the teddy bear. *Of course. What room of Vincent's would be complete without Martin? Thank God Grandma thought to pick him up - I completely forgot. As much as he'd never admit it, Vincent would feel entirely out of place waking up without him.*

And that was it... wasn't it?

No, something else lay at the bottom of the bag, no greater than a receipt, asking for no more attention than a shadow. Anna reached in and felt soft feathers and string wrap around her fingers.

The dreamcatcher. Of course Grandma would bring that goddamn dreamcatcher.

Its fragile frame trembled in her grip. There seemed to be an energy inside it, as if the feathers were urging themselves into flight, as if the string wished to unwind and snake away. The willow body looked as brittle as dried bark, yet utterly, hopelessly eternal.

She held it up to the thin light of the room, watching the web in its centre shimmer. *Just a piece of superstitious junk,* she knew, but Grandma had made her point. Vincent's run of nightmares had been brought to a halt... though sadly not the inevitable trip to the doctors, it seemed.

Psychology. It's all inside his head, see?

If only that wasn't the case, she now wished. As much as Anna felt relieved Vincent had suffered no physical injury - and she would never wish this upon him, of course - part of her knew that cuts, bruises and broken bones would be an easier pill to swallow. That she could relate to; that she could see. But her little boy, her little Vincent lying there like an empty oyster shell, his character drained out -

that she couldn't come to terms with. She didn't believe she ever would.

She peered at Vincent through the gaps between strands of thread. She thought she saw one twitch like a crane fly's spindly leg, torn from its body by a school yard bully, but knew it was just her nerves. Her hands were trembling, adrenaline still fighting through her veins.

She stood up, satisfying that burrowing urge in her gut to do *something*. To stretch her legs, to pace around, to do anything but succumb to that hopelessness. She walked to the window, peered through the blinds into the summer night and sighed.

It all felt so detached.

She picked Martin up by his soft, cushioned paw and realised that she still had the dreamcatcher in her other hand. It looked so innocent next to the teddy, like the toy of a toy. Martin she placed on the chair nearest the bed in mock guardianship; to the dreamcatcher she remained attached.

Part of her wanted to hang it from the clock above the bed, to ward off those evil spirits and dreams that might haunt her son in his perpetual slumber. Where's the harm in that? In doing everything she can? But the other half of her, a much stronger and more desperate half, hated the pathetic futility of it all.

What's the bloody point? she asked herself, feeling the feathers give beneath her fingertips. *What good will it do? To what desperate pits have I plummeted that I hope a preened piece of childish trash, of bloody make-believe, is going to help my son?*

He's in a fucking coma.

The world split into a kaleidoscopic patchwork of decahedrons, sparkling and bleeding into one another. She blinked the tears back, too late to stop one from falling and sinking into the duvet.

Her hand rose with the dreamcatcher, holding it to the clock as it *tick, tick, ticked* its way through the night. Yet suddenly it felt so heavy, like somebody was pulling at her wrist, closing her fingers into a fist. She felt rage, an insatiable urge to hurt and thrash, tightening her skin. Her hairs stood straight and taut. Her boy lay lost and empty before her and here she was, just standing idly as the seconds passed by. Her teeth gritted together, her stomach knotted tight.

Tick. Tick. Crack.

She looked to her palm. A sparrow lay within, its chest crushed, feathers ruffled. It was so frail, so cold, its beak hanging half-open as the last of its breath trickled out.

But then it wasn't a sparrow, only the dreamcatcher, its willow frame cracked like broken bone. String draped freely and feathers pirouetted to the floor. Life was gone; all of a sudden it was nothing but a hollow husk.

She let it slip from her palm. It fell like a jellyfish diving to the seabed, its ravaged tendrils billowing out behind. Bit by bit it fell apart, a meteorite breaking up in the atmosphere and tumbling towards the bin below. It landed amongst the mountains of tissues that had built up over the past few hours.

Anna sat down beside Martin. That burrowing urge to do something had passed and a familiar dread had started to form in her chest, that dark pit far deeper than any cavern, any black hole. She simply wanted to fade away, to cry until the end.

The gulping sobs came back once again, and this time she let them burst forth in full flow. And all the while the dreamcatcher lay shattered, its threads twitching and trembling, releasing whatever nightmares caught within.

CHAPTER NINE

Darkness swam through channels of shadow; oily masses writhed in a violent embrace. All was void, emptiness, nothingness. The black was endless, an infinite oblivion.

Vincent knew he was *somewhere*, but was struggling to find any clues. It worried him that he couldn't tell where the darkness ended and the shadows began, but less so than it did not knowing how close all that blackness was. *Does it ever end? Or is its edge right in front of my nose? Am I blind?*

No, not unless all my other senses have failed too. There is no stimuli here, no sound, no taste, no smell.

At least the panic had subsided. He'd screamed and screamed until exhaustion had overcome him and forced him into silence. He'd accepted his situation, just as he had the white turning to black.

He stretched out his hand, expecting to feel the cold wood of a coffin around him. Nothing. He brought his hand to his face, wondering if perhaps the gloom could be wiped from his eyes. His fingers brushed his skin, and that was something at least. *He* was still a physical entity, if nothing else.

He realised, with the joy of a detective finding the murder weapon at a crime scene, that he could see his hand. The rest of his body too, in fact.

The darkness here isn't the absence of light. It's its own entity, its polar opposite, an all-consuming absolute.

At least he was wearing clothes, and his favourite t-shirt and jeans at that. A wide eyed boy with obscenely purple hair stared out from his top with manic glee, an image torn straight from his favourite comic.

One step forwards, then another. Still he encountered no resistance, not even from the ground below him, for each foot left no impression. It was as if he walked on air.

'Mum?' he cried out, the word cut short as if in a recording booth. 'Anyone?' he continued, again with not even an echo in response.

'Grandma?'

Nothing. It was worth a shot.

'Mum? Hello? Is anybody out there?'

Thinking about it, were the words actually being said or just spelling themselves out in his head?

He still had no idea how much time had passed. Surely it couldn't be minutes; surely it was hours? He thought back to his last math test, where he'd spent what seemed the slightest moment struggling over a question only to glance at the clock and see that five whole minutes had passed. And yet when he'd finished the exam, waiting for it to come to an end, the clock seemed to be running almost backwards.

But on he trudged, for time seemed immaterial.

How far had he travelled? He imagined dragging himself through a desert, the sun passing lazily in the background. He imagined treading water - doggy-paddling just to stay in place.

No up. No down. No bearings. Nowhere to come from, nowhere to go. He let himself slow and then stop, patient like a foetus waiting in the womb. Waiting to be reborn.

'Hey, Vincent.'

CHAPTER TEN

There she was, hair in bunches, wearing her favourite pink petticoat, as pretty as when he saw her last. Her voice carried like petals in a stream, smooth as golden syrup - immediate, yet a million miles away.

Lily stood as if waiting for a bus, eyes impatient yet reluctantly resigned to rest. She pinched the waistline of her dress between her fingers and studied Vincent closely, cocking her head to one side.

'What are *you* doing here?' she said.

Vincent considered this. Nope, he still couldn't quite put his finger on that particular answer. Unless...

'Wait, am I dead too?' he asked.

'Why would you be dead?'

'Well, *you're* dead, so if you're here then-'

'I'm not dead.'

Vincent let his words catch in his mouth, held them there a moment, then continued.

'Are you sure? Because I went to your funeral and I'm pretty sure that's a required factor for the party concerned.'

'Oh Vincent, you're so silly!' She laughed and Vincent felt goosebumps sprout on his arms like the pitter patter footsteps of ants. It was her laugh, alright - a bubbly, almost staccato giggle - yet it was alien, as if somebody had played it through a phonograph or recorded her from another world. A memory, crystal clear.

'How can I be dead when I'm standing right here? Do I look dead to you?'

Some deep, still-developing part of Vincent's mind suspected that this was a loaded question.

'Erm... no, but-'

'Do I not look healthy? Am I not breathing, and talking, and standing right before you?'

'Well, yes, but-'

'Then I'm alive, and I'll hear no more about it.' She stomped her foot and put her hands on her hips in a pretend temper. She even pointed her nose upwards.

'I guess that makes sense...' said Vincent, furrowing his eyebrows. 'Or makes it easier, at least.'

They both continued to stand six feet apart.

'So if you're not dead, and I'm not dead, then where are we? And how do we get home?'

Lily ignored the question.

'Still having your birthday party? Not long now, is it?'

Ah yes, thought Vincent, *the birthday party*. He hadn't thought much about it since the funeral but yes, the invitations had been sent out, the replies received. Eleven years.

'Just a little over a week away,' he said.

'Oh good. I'm looking forward to cake, and party bags... and at least nine balloons!'

like a tape wound back

'-at least nine balloons.'

She was smiling, but it was the artificial grin of a salesman, one you suspected had been practiced and perfected in a mirror. Static and wide.

Vincent shifted from one foot to the other... not that he had any weight to shift in this place.

'Sorry, how do we get home again?'

'We *are* home, Vincent,' she said, arms spread wide. 'Don't you see?'

Vincent did not see. He didn't see anything in fact, save for the swirling darkness, yet Lily was pirouetting around as if dancing in her living room, treading the surface of an oily black lake.

'But how do we get back *home*, Lily? Home with family and friends and school, back to how it was?'

'Oh, there's no going back *there*, Vincent. That's a lifetime ago. Clocks run forward; effects follow cause. Now we're beyond, and there's no returning from here.'

'But there must be a way out,' Vincent cried, searching in every direction. 'If we got *in* here then there must be a way to get *out*. A door opens on both sides, or something like that?'

'Well you can go looking for a door if you want, but I'm not going anywhere. I'm home, don't you see?' She started to step backwards, growing distant from Vincent. 'Home is where the heart is, where my heart belongs is home, and home is where...'

She spun around and skipped away, bouncing up and down like a marionette. Smaller and smaller she grew as her song, a simple, looping melody, grew fainter too.

'Hey, wait! Come back!'

His words fell on deaf ears; still she danced as if through fields of daisies and gold, still she reduced herself to a dot in the distance.

'Lily! Where are you going?'

He shook himself free of his stupor and chased after her. He felt himself barrel through space faster than he could ever imagine, all sense of time and form behind him, yet still Lily remained the tiniest blur of colour on an infinite horizon.

'Lily!' he repeated. 'Come back! I can take you home, I can take us both home!'

He raced towards her, knowing that if he could only reach her, if he could only grab her hand, he could find a way back home for them both. He'd see her hugging her family, their eyes watering with joy; he'd see her back at school, smiling at him from behind her textbook. If he could only catch up to her then everything would be back to how it was supposed to be. Everything would go back to being okay again.

But no matter how fast he ran, no matter how hard he tried or how loud he cried, she only drew further away. He tore through the void yet her merry, skipping figure shrunk and shrunk and... vanished.

'Lily!' he shouted one final time.

He rushed into the darkness, uncertain of where to follow. It continued to writhe around him, coiling itself into mocking shapes amongst the shadows of shadows. She was out there somewhere, hidden behind the obsidian gloom. He pushed himself further, deeper into the dark.

Then suddenly he felt himself falling, having stumbled into something. The world became material and he felt his own weight pour over him as air streamed past his face. It was as if somebody had re-enabled all his senses at once, then strapped him into a gyroscope. Reality had shifted into gear, and was approaching him fast.

He hit the ground and the world faded to colour.

CHAPTER ELEVEN

Three birds perched upon a branch, watching the world grow out before them. They ruffled their feathers and shifted from scraggly foot to scraggly foot, easing their way into the new reality.

The Vultures Three bared witness to deserts rising from nothing like oil springing from the ground, to mountains sprouting like daffodils in an insurmountable mock picket fence. They saw forests of rotten trees claw up like the undead from the earth; they watched twitching scorpions writhe into being with all the finesse of a crab being pulled apart. A stone tower began to climb to the sky, and they saw that too.

'Where's the boy?' came a voice sharp and wild. The words screeched out from the fattest of the three vultures, which sported an appearance that lay somewhere between messy and eccentric. Feathers stuck out in every direction, which only added to an already excessive circumference. The branch bowed under its weight.

'Seriously? You're thinking of food already?' replied the vulture in the middle. This one was the best presented and, all things considered, didn't scrub up too badly. The only things that stopped it from being an attractive bird were its stunted beak, receding featherline and general species.

The third bird, skulking the furthest up the branch, stayed silent, eyeing up the other two vultures with a sort of quiet resentment. It was pock-marked, chipped and looked as if it had survived a plucking. What remaining feathers stuck out did so from a frame little more than skeletal. It appeared that its fatter companion didn't like to share.

'Existing is a hungry business,' the fat one said, shifting guiltily.

'Well get used to that rumbly tummy, because we're not here to eat. Not yet, at least. Not until his majesty has had his fill.'

The other two vultures shivered and arched up their shoulders. A few yellow rocks sprung up into existence around them. A bovine skull joined them for good measure.

The sound of scuffled footsteps interrupted the formation of the sun, which was weaving itself from flaming yarn in the centre of the sky. Two figures, smothered by their cloaks, approached the base of the tree.

'And so it begins,' said the middle vulture, stretching out its blackened wings.

CHAPTER TWELVE

Dirt. That was what taste filled his mouth: dry, crumbling clumps of dirt. He spat it out, scraping mud off his tongue with his teeth. The grit crunched and cracked between them.

He opened his eyes. More dirt. He coughed and it blew up into his pupils like the dust cloud of an atomic bomb. He sat up, blinking until tears washed the stinging away. As he went to wipe the soil from his face, he realised his hands were caked in it too. The air was thick with petrichor, promising life amongst the barren.

He was sat in the middle of a tunnel, one that seemed carved through the very earth. The walls were a dark brown in colour, the tight track worn and flat. Every now and then the tunnel would tremble, and streams of dust and stone would sprinkle from what Vincent loosely defined as the roof.

Where am I? he wondered. *And how did I get here?*

Presumably he was underground, though what ground he was under was anybody's guess. This particular tunnel stretched off into darkness in both directions and, looking up, Vincent could see that he hadn't fallen *from* anywhere in particular. He seemed to have only fallen *to*. He stood up and brushed the dirt from his knees and shins.

There was the faintest scratching beside him, like the writing of tiny chalk against blackboard. He peered at the wall, seeing the soil shake and crawl.

Then out a worm wriggled, plump and content. It glowed from within and suddenly Vincent realised what illuminated the tunnel. In lieu of a sun a thousand of these grubs were burrowing through the earth, their organs shining like lighthouse beacons through translucent skin. This one was particularly fat, gobbling down soil like Vincent would an ice cream sundae.

He reached out, letting it crawl with slow reluctance onto his hand. Inch by inch it crept over his palm, up onto his fingers, then around to the back of his hand. It tickled, like somebody tracing their fingers over the hairs of his arm. He raised his hand back to the wall and the worm-grub stretched itself towards the soil, digging itself a new channel.

Looking down the tunnel was like watching the Christmas lights in the high street come on at night - shiny, yellow bulbs blossoming row by row.

Well, there was no point turning back - or in this case, going down the darker of the two directions. Vincent wasn't sure if the worms were showing him the way or if they simply found the soil ahead more delicious, but at least he'd be able to see where he was going. He set off down the tunnel's slender lane with shaking footsteps.

'Hello?' he shouted.

He heard his voice return, over and over again, and wished he'd never called. Each mimicking echo was a reminder of his aloneness or worse - the possibility that he wasn't alone at all. He tucked his hands under his armpits and pressed on, trying to become as small as possible, if not invisible. Who knew what could lurk around each bend.

He came to a split in the tunnel. Each route looked as endless as the other.

If only there was a signpost, saying 'Safety' one way and 'Danger' the other.

If I had a coin I'd flip it.

He knew it would land heads up anyway, so he went left. It was just as nondescript a tunnel as the last, the same hollow combination of dirt and grubs, marinated in air kept hostage for far too long.

Another junction. This time he turned right.

And on it went. Vincent began to think that there was no way out, that he had been placed within a labyrinth with no entrance or exit. An isolated, impenetrable, unsolvable maze. And it went on for a great deal longer, before his skin started to crawl like the grubs in the walls.

A small ball of ivory sat amongst the dirt, pocked with craters and cracks. It gleamed like the sole star in a night's sky. Vincent picked it up, flinching at the cold, wet film that smothered it, and turned it over.

He dropped it to the earth with a start.

The skull of an infant stared back at him through filthy sockets. Worms, disturbed, wriggled through the holes. Vincent was sure it would have been grinning, had it still possessed a jaw. Instead its teeth sank back into the soil, resembling a skeleton breaking through the earth.

So small. It looks so small.

Who had come before? Who, before, had found it impossible to escape? He felt a river of sweat run into the small of his back.

This isn't a maze. This is a prison.

Lily was somewhere in here, skipping through the tunnels like Little Red Riding Hood, blissfully unaware of the wolves that followed. Or perhaps she cowered in a corner, head tucked between her knees, crying with a dawning realisation that there *is no way out.*

Hold on Lily. I can save you. I can get us both out of here, I promise.

But the further he continued down the path, the more he wanted to race back the way he came. At one point he nearly fell again, this time stumbling over an old, decaying root that had twisted its way out from the earth. Like a witch's hand it had caught him by the ankle, almost sending him head over heels.

Through tunnel and tunnel he passed, following identical walls as he turned left, then right, then left. Always the same collage of browns and lights, browns and lights. Some had claw-like scratchings etched into them; some were smooth. He wasn't sure if he was even seeing the way anymore, or simply so blinkered in his vision that moving forwards was the only option. Once more he could have sworn he'd been walking for hours, only this time his legs were feeling the strain. Hot and heavy; it felt as if somebody had drilled holes into his calves and filled them with molten lead.

Tired, he dragged himself around the following corner, only to stop as a cold, trickling panic ran down his spine.

The skull of an infant looked back at him, filthy, worm-infested eye sockets and all. The same skull as before. And this time Vincent was *sure* it was grinning.

He couldn't be going round in circles. He couldn't be. He'd very deliberately been going left, then right, then left, for the very reason that he knew to stick to one direction would result in looping around and around. He wasn't going in circles. He wasn't *stupid*.

It can't be the same skull. That's it - it's got to be. Being stuck down here is playing tricks on my mind. My eyes are strained; my brain's running on empty. It's just another skull, laughing at me.

The head kept its stare.

He edged past it with his back to the wall, trying to avoid any unnecessary eye-to-socket contact.

Perhaps the walls *were* the same. It was difficult to tell. He needed to stop, yet he couldn't help but press forward.

Something caught his eye, a movement in the periphery. He was sure that a root, gnarled and knotted, had retreated back into the very earth from which it reached. One second it had been just hanging there, the next it was gone. Back under his armpits his hands went, and up hunched his shoulders.

There it was again. A scampering movement in the shadows, a root scurrying back to its source. He *knew* he saw it that time. Were these roots all from the same twitching tree? Was he trapped beneath a massive, living forest? He thought back to the root that tripped him up, and shuddered.

He screamed as something dropped onto the top of his head.

Frantically running his hands through his hair he pulled out a tiny spider, no greater than a wristwatch's face in size. It was pedalling desperately with seven of its legs. Vincent hoped the eighth wasn't still writhing about on his scalp, and dropped the poor creature to the floor.

He looked up and saw thousands of tiny hairs sprouting from the ceiling, a carpeting wave that sent down billows of dust and spun the air brown. From there hundreds - nay, thousands - of spiders flooded the tunnel, each as small as the first, scuttling over one another down the walls and across the floor in an all-devouring swarm. Their tapping sounded like machine gun fire from a mile away.

Before Vincent could think to run they pooled over his feet, drowning his trainers with their frail, maladroit bodies. They piled ever higher as more dropped down onto his shoulders; he could feel their pin-like legs tickle his skin as they wriggled their way under his clothes.

When he did finally break free he felt them slip away with ease, and winced when he felt them crush underfoot. Their pathetic frames crumbled with every step - *crunch, crunch, crunch* - and spun through the air when he brushed them from his shoulders.

He ran with blood pumping in his ears, the slow thudding drowning out the thundering drone of footsteps behind. The faint taste of iron invaded the recesses of his mouth. He ran faster than he'd ever run in his life, but in the corner of his eyes he could see their legs reaching into his vision. He wasn't running fast enough.

The tunnel ahead grew dense, smothered by a netted mass that devoured the light of the glowing grubs ahead. The roots were back and more vicious than ever, twisting their way from the earth like thick, black snakes. They were out to grab him, trip him up, drag him back into the soil.

Further out they reached, yet Vincent knew he could not stop. Not for the spiders behind or the roots beyond. But it was then that he realised that the roots were not roots at all, but instead the crooked, hairy legs of the largest, most grotesque arachnids Vincent had ever seen.

Like dogs they ran through the tunnel towards him, a pack descending on its prey. So large were they that they spilled into all available space, almost tumbling as one gigantic ball like the boulder in *Raiders of the Lost Ark.* Each of their legs was as wide as a beer bottle, their fangs snapped like the pincers of lobsters, and their eyes, assembled like kaleidoscopic rubies, shone red against their jet-black coats.

Nest. I'm in a nest. They're here to spin me up in silken twine, to melt my guts and break my spine.

He couldn't stop, lest he be swallowed by the wave of tiny spiders behind. He imagined them suffocating his skin, crawling over his eyes, flooding into his mouth until they filled him up inside. But even that seemed preferable to the lacerating carnage promised by the beasts ahead. He could hear the clacking of their fangs, the thudding as their legs stamped through the earth.

Yet suddenly the tunnel wasn't a single path after all, but rather forked in two directions. The pulsing in his temples had distracted him, forcing his vision forward but there it was, as clear as a summer sky and just as inviting. If he could only make it there before becoming arthropod chow.

Even as he used the last of his energy to sprint ahead he felt spiders fall from the ceiling like pennies in an arcade machine, piling upon him in an attempt to weigh down his arms and shoulders. They leapt upon his shoes, pulling at the laces. They built themselves into ladders, stretching up the back of his t-shirt. Despite their tiny size, they were slowing him down.

He reached the fork in the tunnel at the same time as the first of the larger beasts, but he was that little bit quicker. He kicked out as he passed, his foot landing amongst its various legs and mandibles with a dull thud. The spider flipped backwards, still flailing its limbs, and the other spiders sprinted over without pause.

Vincent was already halfway down the next tunnel. His stomach heaved with exhaustion, his eyes strained to the point of bursting, but he wasn't about to let any eight legged critter turn him into lunch.

Brown passing brown, Vincent suddenly realised that it wasn't all the same; his world was getting brighter and brighter. From bistre to burgundy and sienna to sand, the soil around him was getting lighter as he ran. It wasn't the wriggling worms in the walls either. With a realisation dawning like the creeping sun at morn he knew he was coming to the end of the labyrinth.

He was coming *home.*

But the storm behind is growing closer.

And it was, too; a thousand legs crashed through the earth like a storm cloud, dust billowing all around. Closer, ever closer.

For some reason his mind wandered back to Harrington Primary School's Sports Day, which had taken place the year just passed. It travelled to the moment that he was winning the relay race, a brief moment but a moment nonetheless, when he could hear all the other runners just inches behind him. Despite the cheers and support of classmates and parents alike, all he could hear was the battering pace of Mike Atherton's trainers closing the distance. The fastest boy in the year, Vincent knew Mike would overtake him before he reached the finishing line. He just had to hold out for as long as he could, which, in the case of Vincent versus Mike, hadn't been very long at all. He wouldn't be falling behind this time though, no sir.

He found one last surge of adrenaline and fled into the light, hoping to each and every god that something good, something safe, lay on the other side.

He almost stopped running in time.

The path ended at the lip of a vast cavern, its cliff-like walls peppered with the openings of tunnels identical to his own. Had Vincent not been preoccupied with swinging his arms around in a comic attempt to keep himself from falling, he would have remarked on how it resembled what he imagined the inside of a beehive to look like.

Momentum pushed him forwards and he tumbled into the pit below. Round and round the cavern spun, the hundreds of holes running into one another like ink. If up was up and down was down, he could not tell the difference.

He stopped far more abruptly than he had fallen, yet Vincent realised with a slow suspicion that his back did not seem broken. In fact, he felt no pain at all; what alarmed him instead was that nothing of his seemed willing to move.

Oh god, that's it. I've broken my spine in two. I'm paralysed.

Nope, his fingers waggled fine. His eyes could roll in their sockets.

He tried to lift his head, and found he could raise it just enough to look to either side. What first appeared as a great expanse of white then split into ribbons and streaks, networking across one another in a net that spanned the entire width of the cavern. Below him the cliffs continued downwards, into a chasm of eternal black.

He was stuck against a spider's web greater than any he could imagine.

His shirt was held against it as if by glue, pulling away from his skin and throttling his neck as he tried in vain to sit up. The same with his trousers; it was like trying to stand with boardwalk planks strapped to each leg. He was pretty sure his shoe had slipped off, because the air felt very cold through his sock.

At least the spiders weren't following. Natural light poured through a hole in the tip of the cavern, and through its rays he could spot nothing more than the occasional spindly appendage pointing out from the tunnels above.

His eyes stung against the sun. He lowered his gaze and returned to struggling against the web's vice-like grip.

A shadow passed overhead. A *big* shadow.

Vincent looked up, with all the speed of sticky treacle.

With the steady measure of a wolf in the hunt, with legs as wide as tree trunks, with a torso the size of a bungalow, with clustered eyes so large Vincent could see his snow-white face reflected, it descended.

With the majesty of a queen upon a throne, lowered by silk as thick as an elevator cable, knocking boulders of dirt from the walls as if they were made of soft cake, it descended.

Face to face it drew, the greatest spider Vincent had ever seen. Greater than he could even fathom. It crawled towards him, each of its eight legs working effortlessly to cross the web. He tried to break free, but still he was stuck fast.

Face to face it drew, until he could feel its hairs against his face, until he could smell its earthy odour fall upon him, until all he could hear was the cracking of its pincers.

Clack. Clack. Clack.

CHAPTER THIRTEEN

It leered forwards, its enormous body blotting out the light from above. All Vincent could see was his own face, reflected tenfold in its eyes. Near jet black with vicious flecks of red, the stain of dead worms could be smelled upon its breath.

The hairs on its pincers brushed at Vincent's face.

'Well, what do we have here?'

The voice sloshed off the walls of the cavern, filling its cracks like golden honey. It was feminine, regal, dignified.

Vincent slowly opened one eye, then immediately closed it.

A couple of seconds later he dared peer out again. The giant spider was still standing over him, its mandibles clapping together with curiosity. Its head was tilted to the side.

'I- I'm sorry?' Vincent mustered.

'I said, haven't you found yourself in a sticky situation?' came the same sweet voice.

'Eat him!' shouted down a shrill, scratchy voice from above. A number of the smaller spiders had ventured to the ends of their tunnels, and were watching hungrily.

'No, don't eat me!' shouted Vincent, once again struggling in vain to break free from the glue-like webbing. It was like quicksand; it only seemed to make things worse. 'I'm small and thin, you'll only get bone!'

'Eat him!' the same voice cried again.

'Wrap him in twine!' came an eager shout from the other end of the cavern.

Then the whole hive was filled with a hundred voices, each as sharp as the first and singing in unison. 'A fly will fly its name implies, yet in our web it simply dies. A fly will fly-'

'Silence!' roared the giant spider, clicking its pincers. All the smaller spiders stopped mid-song and edged back into the shadows of their tunnels. Their colossal counterpart turned back to Vincent, and he could be sure there was sympathy in those many eyes.

'My children, not everything that falls into the web must be consumed! And what a gift has been bestowed upon us today, what a gift!'

It brushed its feelers across Vincent's face like the brushes at a car wash.

'For I believe - and correct me if I'm wrong - that this here boy is *Vincent*. This here boy is the *Source*.'

A hushed silence washed over the insectoid hall. Somewhere a spider with a weak disposition fainted.

'Hold on one minute,' said Vincent, still unsure exactly how to approach talking to a spider. 'How do you know my name?' He had the unnerving suspicion that, if he could move, he would be kneeling. There was an aura around this creature that reminded him of the Queen of England.

'I don't know your name. *You* know your name. Or rather, I know your name because you know your name, and that's all that matters really. Make sense?'

Vincent was quite sure that it didn't.

Another tilt of the head from the spider. 'You really don't know where you are, do you?'

Vincent hazarded a shake of the head.

'Oh boy, you are far from home aren't you? Or rather as close as one can get to it.'

'I'm... I'm dead, aren't I?'

The spider laughed, which as anyone can imagine was considerably disturbing. It was like a hiccup cut into thirds.

'Oh, far from it! We'd all be in trouble if that was true, at any rate. No, we're only here because you're very much alive.'

'Oh god,' moaned Vincent, and would have covered his face with his hands if he'd been capable of moving them. His mind swam in circles. 'But where is here?'

'Ah, good question. This,' she replied, gesturing with her front two legs to the surrounding walls, 'is the world of dreams and nightmares - the Nation of Rooma, if you will. As familiar as your hallway stairs in the day, as alien as those same stairs come night.'

This didn't rescue Vincent's drowning mind all that much.

'Then how did I get here? Last thing I remember is coming home from the shops with Mother...'

you're not a bloody baby, twisting metal, you're not a bloody baby, screeching metal

'...oh no, no this isn't alright, I need to get out of here, I need-'

'Calm down,' said the spider, putting the tip of one surprisingly light leg against his chest. 'You're not going anywhere just yet. And regardless, you still haven't worked out where here *is*, it seems.'

'...but you said this is the Nation of Rooney-'

'Rooma.'

'-yes, Rooma. So that's it, right? Follow a path and go home, go home to Mother?'

'Ah, sweet boy. If only it was that easy! You're in a world where no map exists, where there is no set path to follow. You are-,' the spider lifted her leg from Vincent's chest and tapped him on the forehead, '-here.'

A moment of expectant silence.

'What?' replied Vincent.

The spider rolled her various eyes.

'You're asleep. Well, sort of. The big sleep, as it were. No, not like that,' she added, noticing what remaining colour Vincent had in his face drain away, 'you're not dead. Just... in a coma.'

'W-What? Coma? Oh god, everything's gone horribly wrong!'

'Oh don't be so *melodramatic,*' the spider said, holding her front-most legs parallel to her face in mockery. 'It could be worse. You could be a figment of imagination existing only in the temporary mindscape of a coma patient. One could easily succumb to an existential crisis, you know.'

'Eurgh.'

'Exactly.'

'So none of this is real then? It's all just make believe?'

'Oh Lord no,' replied the spider, appalled. 'Quite the opposite, dear boy. Is there anything more real than what resides within your mind? Do I not appear real to you?'

She leered closer with one massive, crimson eye.

Vincent coughed nervously. 'I suppose so... but who are you, exactly?'

'Oh my manners,' the spider said, covering her mouth with one terrible leg. 'Please forgive me. I am the Mother Spider,' she said, curtseying as much as her enormous frame would allow, 'and all these are my children. Welcome, to our humble abode.'

'Well thank you, and a very nice home it is too,' he added, surveying the crumbling cavern walls, 'but I really should be going. My own mother will be worried sick and, if this is all inside my head, I'd very much like to go home now. If it's all the same to you.'

'Oh, of course! Far be it from us to keep you here. But it's not as simple as just strolling out the door and waking up in your bed, all fresh as a daisy and pushing up none. No sir. You barely know the what, let alone the why or the how. You might want to calm your horses and just *listen.*'

Oh here we go, thought Vincent. *Sounds like one of Grandma's lectures.*

'Okay, okay. Fine. Consider all my ears open. But there's one thing I need you to do first.'

'Of course, Vincent. Whatever do you need?'

'If it isn't too much of an inconvenience, could you please cut me free?'

* * *

Vincent wiped the remaining residue of webbing from his shirt as he watched Mother Spider repair her web. She'd snipped him free from his sticky trap with ease, and was now stitching together the loose threads. His mind wandered to his Grandma, always knitting, always clicking those clattering needles together.

He now stood at the bottom of the cavern of which the walls, upon a series of clicking noises from Mother Spider, had blossomed with the same glowing grubs as before. Vincent felt as if in a cinema theatre - tiny lights in the walls and floor drowned by an awesome light ahead.

'Mother Spider? Mother Spider?'

She looked down at him in the manner of one looking over half-rim spectacles.

'Yes, Vincent?'

'My horses are calmed and my ears are peeled right open. So *how* am I supposed to get out of this place?'

Mother Spider sighed. 'If only that was as easy to answer as ask. No, the real question is *why* you're in this place at all.'

Silence.

'Well then, *why* on Earth am I in this place?' he asked.

'Well, only you know that. Luckily that also means that I know it, even if you're too stupid to work it out for yourself. I know for a fact that you remember the darkness.'

She was right; no matter where he looked Vincent could still sense that swirling, inky void flowing behind his eyes. The endless, blinding black.

'Well that, boy, is the stuff of nightmares,' Mother Spider continued. 'A pure, liquid dread that pours through every crack and fills every hole. It's no ordinary darkness though, oh no; this darkness drowns out all light in its path until there's nothing but emptiness. You had trouble sleeping, yes?'

Vincent nodded. Each and every night he'd fallen asleep just fine, only to wake up screaming his way out of that terrible graveyard scene.

'That was the darkness trying to break loose. It comes at night to pierce your dreams, feeding off the light. It's the only way he can be free, the only time he can escape the periphery. That's why the Ojibwe - sorry, *dreamcatcher* - was so important. Smart woman, your Grandma. It caught all those nasty nightmares before they ever reached your pretty little head. Until it found itself broken, that is...'

'Sorry, can we backtrack a moment? *He?*' interjected Vincent. 'What do you mean, *he?* Are you saying there's somebody else in here with me? Inside *my head?*'

'Not physically of course, that would be ridiculous! Walking around, treading on all your synapses. No, but the idea of him is certainly present. Always is, really. He's the Dark One, the King of Terrors, and he rules Rooma. We're in your head, Vincent, but it's his world you're stuck in.'

'What?' Vincent shouted, clasping his head with both hands. 'Well... get him out! What does he want?'

'Oh, nothing much. Just to drain you of all light, leave you an empty husk, and drown you in darkness.'

'Oh, so nothing too much to worry about at all!' Vincent paced back and forth in the dirt. 'I'll just sit here and let him turn me into nothing but snakeskin and echoes then, shall I? What do I do? *How do I get home?*'

'Those horses don't seem all too calmed to me, young man,' said Mother Spider, climbing down from the web. It was like talking to a house on stilts. 'You can't very well just stroll out there like a Superman. You wouldn't know where you were, where you were supposed to be going, or what to bloody well do. You wouldn't last five minutes by yourself.

'You, Vincent, must travel to the Dark One and stop him. Don't ask me how,' she added, seeing that familiar mask of frustration fold over Vincent's face, 'only you can discover that. You'll find him across the desert, far from here. Far from *you*. All I can tell you is that you need, and you already *know* you need, to find the light. His darkness spreads, and it grows stronger with every second you remain here. He'll want to keep you trapped here for as long as he can, until he's good and fat - but you're not going to let him, are you boy?'

'No, ma'am,' he replied, trying to wrap his head around everything. It didn't seem to have the malleability. A light popped on amongst the clutter, however. 'Wait, if this is all in my head then I'll be fine. This is all make-believe. I'll just find this chump, give him the old one-two - *bam, bam, bam* - and I'll wake up before I know it! You can't die in a dream!'

If Mother Spider could have slapped her forehead in exasperation, she would have.

'Oh, Vincent. Don't you watch films, or television? Ever try reading a book? Of *course* you can die in a dream. Is something in your mind any less real, just because you can't touch it? No, it's *more* real, that's what. Does a man not turn into a husk when his aspirations are extinguished, when his dreams perish? So can a nightmare render you dead.' She leaned in close, her voice suddenly a couple tones deeper. 'A mind can remain bright without a body, but not so well the reverse.'

'So if I die inside here, I die in the real world?'

'The *physical* world, yes. Mind dies, body follows. I wouldn't worry about it though,' she added flippantly, 'you're so unlikely to be dead, not when you're alive. And it's in the Dark One's best interests to keep you breathing anyway.'

A grub burrowed out from the earth by Vincent's feet, seemed to giggle, then buried itself back underground.

'Not necessarily in one piece,' Mother Spider added, 'but breathing all the same.'

Wind whistled through one of the tunnels like an icy scream.

'Lily!' exclaimed Vincent, eyes wide as if he'd seen a ghost. He'd forgotten all about her, about chasing her through the grimy, writhing darkness. She was in here somewhere. He just had to find her.

'Lily!' repeated Vincent. 'She's out there, all alone - the Dark One, I've seen him! He stole her! He crept up through the inky black, with his hands like willow branches and stole her into the deep!'

'Vincent,' said Mother Spider with the slow patience only age and experience brings, 'you do know Lily is dead, don't you?'

'Yes, of course. I'm not an idiot. But I saw her, I saw her running and I chased so I know she's...'

'She's dead, Vincent. She isn't here. I know you saw her, but she isn't here.'

'If I can find her I can bring her back. If I can make it home, so can she.'

'It doesn't work like that, Vincent. You're here. You're *actually* here - this is your mind. She's just a memory.'

'No. No, I don't believe you. I'll find her and I'll get her home. It'll be as it was. Surely it's worth a shot, at least?'

'No, Vincent. No, I really don't think it is.'

But Vincent wasn't listening; his mind was as made as a bed in Claridge's, reassured in its plush comforts. He'd seen her grow distant to the size of a dot, a pink speck in the obsidian gloom. It was burnt into his retinas. He would find her, and he would bring her home.

'Well, we'd better get you on your way,' said Mother Spider. 'You've wasted enough time listening to me prattle on. We'll get you to the Dark One's tower... and home before you know it,' she added, noticing the glassed expression of Vincent's eyes.

She pushed him towards a tunnel with one of her powerful forelegs. It was like being moved forward by the mechanism that knocks down the pins at bowling alleys; his legs struggled to keep him upright. It took his fluffy mind a few seconds to notice that something approaching a natural light was very nearly succeeding in illuminating their path.

'Wait, how am I to cross this desert? I'm no slow-poke but I somehow doubt I'm going to make it across the Sahara, dream or no dream.'

'Oh, you won't be walking,' Mother Spider replied, stifling a chuckle like twigs being snapped underfoot. 'No, that would never do.'

And that was when he heard it - or rather, felt it. A thick vibration in the earth, the heavy sound of weight and power.

CHAPTER FOURTEEN

His eyes grew wide as he approached the noise and the engines. If there's a way into many a man's imagination it's a big engine, and Vincent, being but a boy, was impressed tenfold. Before him quaked a motor of Victorian style and excess.

It stood four storeys high or more, all thrusting pistons and grinding gears, its clattering belts drowned by the lion's roar of its dozen generators. Sparks burst forth in glittering showers, and dynamos popped and exploded with bombast.

Before him chugged a colossal, goliath, monstrously grandiose steam engine.

It wasn't a train as such. No, despite its railway wheels - each taller than a shire horse - the rows of carriages looked more a weapon of war than any locomotive Vincent had ever seen. It was a railcar with which to ram the gates of hell. It was offensively big.

It looked defensively big, too.

Housed in a second enormous cavern, resting against buffers the size of boulders, the engine pumped out steam and smoke so thick that a cloud system had formed against its chamber's roof. The odd drip of water fell from above, hissing as it splashed upon hot metal. Squinting, Vincent was sure he could make out silhouettes of birds with huge wingspans, swooping through the mist. The train's track ran ahead into a gaping, pitch-black tunnel.

'The Rooma Express. Modest, isn't it?' said Mother Spider, walking past him into the cavern. 'They wanted it to be bigger, but we simply couldn't get the manpower.'

'Oh yeah, very subtle. What on earth does it run on, nuclear fusion?'

Mother Spider looked at him, mouth agape. 'Nuclear? My god no. That's far too dangerous. Good old fire and elbow grease, of course. Good for the disposition.

'Not that you'll be doing any work, of course. You'll be riding in comfort. It might not look it from down here, but the interior is actually rather lovely.'

Vincent wasn't about to call her out, but he found it difficult to believe that Mother Spider had ever been inside. Huge as the carriages were, she'd fill out every room like a cat squeezed into a vase.

'I'll believe it when I see it.'

'You'll see it when you believe it, if you think about it.'

If it isn't already obvious, being trapped in one's own head is a rather confusing affair. The subconscious tends to feel superior over the conscious, pointing and making fun. Vincent was choosing to ignore it; his mind was too smart for its own good.

A horn more suited to a ship in fog blew out, and more pistons began to pump, more dynamos popped. The train was ready to leave, heaving against its brakes like a tiger ready to pounce from its cage.

'Right, better get you onboard then,' said Mother Spider, picking Vincent up with two of her enormous, hairy legs. It was like being lifted by carpeted logs. She placed him high up on the metal steps outside what appeared to be the passenger quarters, behind a railing that was brown and flaked with rust. He brushed his clothes down without thinking, but she appeared not to notice.

'Remember, Vincent,' she called out as the train's wheels came to life, 'the path of the past is a tempting one, but hidden 'neath the roses and lilies lie land mines and bear traps. No man can change that route, only risk its journey. Better to stomp out a path ahead, keep your head down, and mind your feet stay in the present.'

The train began to pick up speed.

'Oh, and one more thing!' shouted Mother Spider, scuttling after him. 'Watch out for the Pale One. He'll be out there too, somewhere.'

'How do I find him?' Vincent called back.

'You don't find him. He'll come to you, as he does us all.'

The wind whipped around his hair as the train slipped into the tunnel. The air was stale and dark.

He sighed against the door of the carriage. Things had got bloody weird.

CHAPTER FIFTEEN

Amongst the cold, windswept stone he waited, accompanied by the lonely, whistling gales that echoed through his castle chamber like ghosts trapped in a waltz. Far above and from Rooma his tower snaked into the sky, a serpent rising to his tune brick by bloody brick.

The Dark One was alone. He liked it that way.

'How long must I wait in these wretched halls?' he asked no-one in particular, in a voice as deep as a black hole and twice as dark. 'A King of Terrors they proclaim me, yet what king is king with a kingdom gone? This world slips like ice and breaks like levees overflowed.'

He rose from a granite throne and paced before it, his long, spindly fingers draping behind his back in a mock cape. The blank void of his face shimmered in the moonlit dark.

For a being so eternal, this world felt so damn *temporary*.

The tower shook as it built itself another storey taller. Had the Dark One hung paintings on the walls they would have fallen, but nothing adorned the room save a deep crimson carpet that ran from the doorway to the throne for appearance's sake. All else was solid, crushing stone, save for the two oak doors that swung open that very moment.

Two hooded figures walked into the chamber. One passed over the floor as if hovering. The other bowled forwards, all knees and elbows... mostly because it *was* all knees and elbows. They were creatures from the Nightmare realm, assembled through chance and chaos.

'Master,' said the first robe-clad visitor in a voice like sandpaper scraped on the buzzing of bees. 'We have reason to believe that the Boy has arrived in Rooma. And...'

'And? Out with it, cretins. Must I bathe in the incompetence of others...'

'And it appears he's travelling aboard the Express train, sir,' came a voice from the other hood. The words didn't so much flow forth as fall with a leaden thump.

Daggers of white split from the darkness, tearing into a Cheshire grin. The two shrouded figures backed ever so slightly away.

'Good, good. An interesting development. See to it that our guest has a pleasant journey, and alights at the appropriate destination.'

The Dark One paced over to the window. Each hood turned to the other, and the second shifted awkwardly.

'Are my words that spill forth of foreign tongue? Begone!' he shouted, waving at them with garden rake fingers.

They bowed, then hurried from the room. The two doors closed behind them with a hollow clunk and silence once more took residence.

He liked it that way.

Rooma stretched out beneath him, a patchwork quilt of dreamscape. From his tower to the mountain range to that blasted spider's nest, all was his. Each grain of desert sand; that was his. Each drop of salted rain; that was his. Each miserable, crawling wretch upon the earth, *his* earth; that was his.

He looked up to the sky, to the swirling vortex of dark clouds that circled his tower like vultures around the dying. Since the boy had arrived, heralded by the burst of light from which this world had also been born, it had grown from a thin smog to quite the modest nebula. Little sparks crackled in its heart.

This world wasn't enough, not for the Dark One. Not for a King. No fruits would grow here, no sir, no matter what fruits they were. He needed more, and he knew just where to find it. With every second that cloud grew greater; with every second that boy wandered the plains he felt himself grow a little stronger. And when the time came, when the darkness had spread across the entire land, he would take it. He would take it all.

A money spider crept along the cold stone of the window sill. The Dark One slammed his fist down upon it, feeling its body flatten and its legs split apart, twitching. Those smiling daggers tore through the black once more.

'Come hither, little boy,' he said, 'and let night fall before the day is done.'

CHAPTER SIXTEEN

The cabin was plush and grand, dripping with taste and balanced on just the right side of pretentiousness. The seats were so soft Vincent could imagine himself falling through them like marshmallow. He would have curled up for a nap had he not been asleep already.

Two velvet curtains were tied back from the window. The tunnel beyond waved various shades of black as they whizzed past. All of the interior was either the same purple cushion or deep brown wood, the kind that Vincent imagined decorated the carriages of Victorian millionaires. Unnecessary expense, that's what it exuded.

Still, Vincent thought, *First Class is always worth having when it's free.*

The thundering of the wheels was but a gentle clock ticking from inside his room. Soundproofed too, it seemed. Vincent could have spun plates, the room was so steady. A single bulb of light hung from the ceiling, flickering gently, humming to itself.

'Look at me, living the life of luxury,' he said to nobody in particular. He beckoned to a pretend waiter. 'I will have the champagne and my partner shall enjoy a glass of red, if you'd be so kind.'

Every other cabin had been empty when Vincent had entered the passenger's quarters. Down the corridor he had walked, identical rooms on either side. Always the same purple velvet, always the same polished wood. He'd chosen this one at random, room 4. Seemed as good as any.

Art deco arches had stood over the doorways, all triangles and polygons like the New York Chrysler. They glistened like gold in the melancholy light. Matching handles reached out from the double doors, inviting him to slide them aside. He'd pulled them shut behind him.

Few minutes had passed, but already Vincent was starting to feel lonely, abandoned. It's a solemn thing, an empty train. As if the other seats should be occupied, as if the sole rider is intruding on a party of ghosts.

Suddenly a burst of light shone through the window, a picture of blinding white. Vincent peered out from under his hand, trying to make sense of the pale yellow that grew.

The desert stretched out before him, tracking past like spokes in a bicycle wheel. In glimpses he caught cacti flexing their arms, earth cracked apart like icebergs in the ocean. He thought, just for a second, that he saw a scorpion as large as a dog scuttle through a hole in the dunes. A scolding sun drifted across a sea of pale azure.

It was endless and it was hostile and it felt like far from home.

Anyone who's ever run away, anyone who's ever tried to get as far away as possible, knows the feeling of growing further and further from what's secure. They know the lightness of the stomach, the fluttering of the heart, the knowledge of the swelling unknown. These were all too apparent to Vincent, who wished only for somebody else to be riding coach beside him.

It felt too much like being shepherded away.

Who was the Spider to send him this way? Who was anyone to tell him what to do, in his own mind of all places? He never made his own decisions. He didn't know where he was going, he didn't know what he was doing, he was stumbling around in the dark. And God only knew where Lily was.

If this was his mind, he'd do what he damn well pleased.

He stared at the empty bench in front of him. His feet seemed reluctant to reach the floor.

Well. He'd find out where he was headed, at the very least.

He got to his feet, took another glance out at the desert rushing by, and slid open the doors. They skipped along their rollers with a whispered rush.

The corridor beyond was empty still. Despite the light from the windows a faint gloom had befallen the aisle. Silence swept along its length, the train of her long, white dress cascading out behind her. The sole other passenger, Vincent felt compelled to know from what she ran.

A deep plum carpet ran the entire stretch from door to door. One door led back out to the railings where Mother Spider had dropped him off, the other to rooms unknown. That way it would be, then.

Putting me on a train and expecting me to stay put, like a cat on its way to the vets. Huh. The cheek of it.

He walked down the corridor, expecting a conductor to burst through the door at any moment and demand a reason as to why Vincent wasn't sitting patiently in his cabin. *Just looking for the bathroom, sir.* What would a conductor here even look like? Would his mind recreate the official of the 12:03 train he took to town with his mother, or even the grumpy old hag that always seemed to frequent the return journeys? Hell, would it even be human at all? Mother Spider hadn't been, obviously. Would it be tendrils and tentacles and eyes, all held together by nothing but wishful thinking, reaching out to stamp his ticket? He shuddered at the thought.

The doors to his right slid open with a slam.

Vincent's heart tried to break through his ribs, hammering for freedom. He wanted to run but he stayed where he was, peering through the doorway with all the subtlety of a stalking cat. The room was empty.

Must have been the rocking of the carriage, thought Vincent, aware of how smooth the ride was. *A gust through the window, perhaps.*

Or perhaps a ghost wandering the halls, an ethereal passenger on his journey through the underworld.

Something told him that the carriage grew just that little bit darker.

Not a horn blew out, not a bird did cry; only his footsteps tapped against the floor. He could sense somebody, some bodies perhaps, watching from beyond sight.

The corridor seemed to run forever, but soon enough Vincent had a hand upon the handle. The door trembled in his grip; whatever lay beyond wasn't privy to whatever secrets of stability this cabin kept.

He had a suspicion that he was leaving the familiar behind again.

He turned the handle and the door swung open. He slipped through the gap without so much as a glance behind.

CHAPTER SEVENTEEN

Vincent thought he knew how they got the passenger cabins so quiet. All the noise had been kept prisoner in here. Every noise there ever was, apparently.

If a whale could shout, a jet could scream and a star belch, still they could not have drowned out the all-encompassing din that welcomed the boy. And the heat; Vincent had felt nothing like it, not even in that summer when he got sunburn and had to stay indoors else everyone see him peel. Sweat ran off him in rivers and each breath felt like taking a bite from the Sahara.

This side of the corridor had none of the splendour of the other; gone were the varnished woods and the velvet curtains; gone were the windows and the rooms. Gone was the stability; the hall shook like a bull at the rodeo. It was vibrant, violent and alive. It was also little more than a tin can, a corrugated iron shaft.

He walked down its length, noticing the shallow decline. The heat grew more intense. The noise deafening.

And when he reached the corridor's end, he knew why.

Six furnaces sat within an enormous metal chamber, each bulging like the belly of the beast, each spitting fire like cackling drunks. Two men worked at each; a dozen bronze and bloody bodies shovelling coal in jerky, animatronic thrusts. Shovel, twist, load; shovel, twist, load. Black stone lay piled up in mountains.

Steam rose up through fat copper pipes, one fed from each furnace, collecting together in the centre of the ceiling. Water dripped like the ticking of a clock, each drop hissing like acid against the metal floor. If the workers were being burned, they did not show it.

Vincent passed between them, ducking under the odd stray ember as it flew across the chamber. It was only when he got closer that he realised each man had an ankle fastened to the floor by a two foot iron chain. Shirtless, their oxen bodies glistened with a thick sheen of sweat. Their faces were as crude as a child's drawing, their eyes glassy and hollow.

They did not seem to see him. Or perhaps they did not care.

Of course, that would have been bad enough. But Vincent had to go and look under his feet.

There was a lot of empty space, under his feet.

The walkway was grated, and what Vincent thought was the floor actually hung in the centre of the chamber, another twenty feet of air stretching out below him. In the darkness, cast in flickering shadows from the furnaces above, sat twenty rows of six men, three to a side. Each had two callused hands on what resembled a knotted tree trunk growing lengthways from the wall, rotating it with heavy, laboured breaths. They looked like vikings stripped of armour, rowing back from battle, covered in blood and cuts.

To the beating of a drum they sang in a steadily rising drone:

> *'Beyond the grave to the grave beyond;*
> *all men follow the one same track.*
> *Don't go looking over your shoulder;*
> *the Pale One watches from out of the black.'*

The words went round and around, swarming out of the mouths of faces blank as canvas. In stark contrast to the low pounding of the timpani came a snapping off-beat whip, cracking across the men's bare backs. Claret ran thick from criss-crossing lacerations but still they kept turning their cranks, grinding the enormous wheels outside along their metal tracks.

One of the men ground to a halt like the ballet dancer in a music box, falling against his handle. The two men to his right continued to push, oblivious to the body as it clattered to the floor. A man draped in a musky brown cloak dragged the lifeless body away by under its arms, and another was brought over in its place. The same colour, shape and face; another clone chained to the floor like all the others.

More whipping, more running red.

It would take a heart colder than coal to not feel sympathy, pity, or desperation for those suffering. Even those that pass the homeless on the street with barely a glance feel a pang of shame in doing so. But now Vincent felt only anger simmering inside. Anger at the pointlessness. Anger at the meaninglessness. And anger at their acceptance of it. The water twitched and spat and soon it would boil. Then out of the pan it would climb, all froth and rage.

That was it. He was getting off this madhouse on wheels. Impending darkness or not, he wasn't going to spend another moment in this hellhole. He didn't care if he had to walk the whole way; he'd just follow the tracks.

A ladder leading to the ceiling lay at the other end of the chamber, past all the furnaces and coal. He rushed to it, and though his footsteps rang out cold against the metal grating no heads turned and no eyes watched. Vincent wondered if it was he, in fact, who was the ghostly passenger.

The rungs were greasy and his fingers slipped, but Vincent hooked his elbows around them one at a time and heaved himself up. Falling from even halfway up would break his back, so he kept his eyes on the prize. Just like climbing the rope in gym class; don't look down.

'...the Pale One watches from out of the black...'

There was a trapdoor in the iron roof, held by a simple latch. Bad luck told him that it would be locked or stuck, yet despite the whisperings in his ear it slipped aside quite freely.

CHAPTER EIGHTEEN

Fresh air. Well, not exactly fresh. Warm, thick air. The sort that feels, as it pours slowly into your lungs, as if it's made the journey a hundred times before. Warm, thick, second-hand air.

The direct sun had its eye on Vincent, and he could feel the back of his t-shirt grow overly fond of his skin. He flapped it to create a breeze, but it only felt more like fly paper upon its return.

The trapdoor had opened up onto the roof of the train. Vincent felt like a mole emerging from its tunnels for the first time, being birthed into a blinding new world. Each breath of that dry, recycled air felt less than satisfying, but the view was quite the opposite.

It stretched out for miles in every direction, an endless expanse of sand and stone. Vincent thought it was beautiful. All sorts of yellows and browns sat amongst one another, gazing up at a perfect, pure blue sky tarnished only by the clouds spewed forth from the engines. The mountain of Mother Spider and her children disappeared behind them until it was little more than a termite's nest in his eyes, but another collection of peaks remained a constant along the horizon. Along the *entire* horizon.

A heavy hand fell upon his shoulder.

'Impressive, ain't it?'

Vincent spun around and looked up into a face like a rocky outcrop. The Grand Canyon seemed to have made residence on both cheeks, and there were more craters than on the dark side of the moon. A bald dome shone under the summer sun and a ring of metal hung from a stubby nose.

'Is it not impressive, boy?' The voice was like boulders falling against one another.

He was torn between two trains of thought. One led him to think of his headmaster, putting a hand on his shoulder and telling him not to run in the corridor else he trip and fall. It spoke of authority, and an obligation to reply in an apologetic tone. The other told him not to talk to strangers, and they didn't come much stranger than this.

'It's very impressive, sir,' he said, leaning away from out of the man's grasp. It seemed like an adequate compromise. 'But... if you don't mind me asking... what is it?'

'Dem's mountains, boy,' replied the man. 'The biggest there is to climb. Called the Big Ridge they are, and you don't ever wanna be crossin' them over. Nuffin' on the other side, or so they say.'

He grinned a grin of two dozen pearly white teeth and the canyons were lost amongst a thousand other cheerful creases.

'Well it's a good thing I'm not going that way then, isn't it,' said Vincent. 'I'm going to the Dark One. I'm going *home*.'

The grin grew tired and dropped away.

'Yes, it seems that way, doesn't it?' He turned and pointed past the front of the train. 'The tracks are headed that way, at least.'

True enough, the two bars of iron ran parallel until they became a dot in the distance. But from that dot grew a massive tower, reaching to the sky like an arthritic finger. And above it was a cloud; a single, black cloud that swirled and spiralled and crackled with fury. Over the roaring of the engines he could just about make out bellowing thunder.

'Is that him?' Vincent asked.

'It's his castle, that's for sure,' said the man, stroking a chin like a cliff. 'All cold and stone. Not what I'd call *home* though. Always struck me as needin' more than four walls, for that.

'What you doin' 'ere anyways? This landscape seems a little too arid for your kind.'

His eyebrows beckoned towards Vincent's t-shirt and trainers with a pointed condescension.

'Seem a bit... foreign.'

'Wha-? *I* look a bit foreign? Have you looked in the mirror recently? Who the hell even are you?'

The man chuckled, laughter rising from his belly and spilling forth like an avalanche. His chest, bare save for tattoo sketching, bounced up and down.

'The Conductor on this 'ere train, that's who I am. I'm exactly where I'm supposed to be. You, however, are not.'

Well, that cleared that up. Unconventional this tribal man might be, but at least he had the correct number of limbs and no tentacles to speak of.

'The passenger cabin was boring,' said Vincent, suddenly paying keen attention to his shoes. 'It seems like I'm the only person on this train. Save for you, of course.'

Blank faces and taut skin rose from his memory.

'Wait, who are all those people down there? Why are they chained up?'

'Ne'er you mind about them, boy,' said the man. 'They're in limbo, doomed to keep these wheels a'turning. They don't really mind. They don't complain, at least. How else do you think we'd get to where we're going?'

'The furnaces! The coal! Like a normal train!'

'Oh, those old things. They're just to keep the turners on their toes. It's easy to get complacent, you know,' he added with a wink. 'Keeps 'em working that little bit harder. High productivity.'

'That's barbaric!'

'That's business, that's what that is.'

Vincent considered the pierced nose, the arms like barrels and the disposition of a dormant volcano. A whip hung from his belt. He decided against pushing the topic.

'Well, mind you stay safe up here, boy,' said the Conductor, bowing slightly. 'I hear the calling of duties and the train won't drive itself. Perhaps you should make yourself acquainted with the other passengers.'

And with that he spun around, marching off towards the front of the train.

When Vincent turned back around he found the train's roof to be awash with cages and cases, each swaying with the rocking of the carriages. They hung from rafters and clashed against one another like metal conkers. Each housed a prisoner like a canary, like freaks at the carny. From one a baby cried, waggling its tiny limbs like a turtle on its back. In another a skeleton sat hunched against the bars, her tattered skin pooled at the base of her cage.

The air was as thick with fear as it was the smell of rot.

Vincent entered the metal forest, ducking under desperate hands that darted from their enclosures. They belonged to bodies frail and hollow, sisters to eyes so gaunt and grey. Naked and emaciated, the prisoners mewled towards this moving, living flesh.

It wasn't long before he came across a familiar face.

'Grandpa?'

There he was, smiling through large, thin-rimmed glasses, that thick, flowing moustache bristling forth in a familiar welcome. Eyebrows so developed they could be considered limbs in their own right. A tweed jacket and beige trousers, wrapped around a wire frame. And if there was any doubt remaining, *Grandpa* was emblazoned on golden plaque at the bottom of his cage. It was him, alright.

He looked down as if without a care in the world which, Vincent supposed, was probably the case. Through his glasses Vincent could see two watery eyes, each a fading electric-blue. How long had it been? Four years? Five? It was like running into an old friend in the street, and being at a loss for anything to say.

'Oh hello, Vincent,' he said. 'Why, haven't you grown! Is it time to play Snakes and Ladders already?'

Vincent felt a tear roll down his cheek. It was half a lifetime ago he'd last seen his Grandpa, and here he was, standing before him as real as flesh and blood. Smiling as if it were yesterday; a rare, kind soul.

'No, it's not time to play yet,' he replied, feeling the words slip out without thought, soft and ethereal.

'Where's Grandma?' he asked, still smiling.

'Grandma's fine, don't worry.' He fought back more tears, struggling to match Grandpa's warm, blissful expression. Struggling. 'She's back home knitting, I'm sure.'

And still a smile stretching to the middle distance.

'Oh hello, Vincent. Is it time to play Snakes and Ladders already?'

That's when the pieces fell into place. Grandpa wasn't here any more than he was; this smiling, beautiful man was assembled from fragments of memory, shards of recollection that glimmered only for a moment before dissipating in a crystalline shower. He could hold on to them but he knew that sooner or later they'd all spill through his fingers, a thousand grains lost amongst the sands of time.

His eyes laced with tears, he forced himself to step away.

Big boys don't cry. Nobody needs tears, save an ocean on a budget.

Another dozen cages, another dozen strangers. The chugging of the train, the rattling of the chains.

A mumbling masked by fog.

The muffled words came from a face distorted and blurred, like one cut from security footage in a police documentary. In white shirt and blue jeans it produced words that swirled and struggled against one another - a dense, warm cloud of pulsating drone. Its pixelated features peered down like a crow from the rooftops, eyeing the boy with blank inquisition.

Vincent recognised something, but what that something was eluded him. It was on the tip of his tongue, just out of arm's reach, at the back of his mind, like when you can't remember what you were about to say. A lead weight sitting there, sweating importance, slowly dissipating into nothing. He knew this man, but from what land or time? Teacher? TV star?

He checked the name plaque at the bottom of the cage but that was distorted too - scratched out as if with a compass. Letters and carvings blended into a deep, chaotic mess. The first letter was a D, perhaps. Maybe an F. Then an A?

A raven smashed against the side of its own cage three rows back, cawing and flapping its wings in the throes of death. Its beak snapped against the iron bars; its scrawny, twig-legs clawed desperately between. When Vincent looked back, the sweat on his spine cold and alien once more, the figure in the cage was gone. All that remained was a mist, pouring through the bars and drifting into the breeze behind in one long, glittering waterfall.

He'd seen enough. A cold hand was prickling the hairs on the back of his neck, and he couldn't help but feel it belonged to one of the many decrepit beings hungry for flesh. Suddenly, surrounded by the crashing of cages and screams of the dead, the silent cabin didn't seem so lonely after all.

He turned back the way he came, but a familiar echo blocked his tracks.

'Hey, Vincent,' came the distant voice, smooth as petals in a stream.

Yes! She was here! Vincent discovered his heart leaping up and hanging on to his tonsils, swinging like a kid on monkey bars. He knew he hadn't lost her. In the pit of his stomach hope had sat, and here she was. She must be amongst the other travellers - *prisoners*, he corrected himself - making their way across the Land of the Dead. She was so close. He would find Lily, and he would bring her home.

He raced between cages as if they were trees in a forest, leaping over cables like snakes that snapped at his ankles. He frantically followed the trail of aural ribbon, pinwheeling its way through the screams and groans.

'Vincent! Vincent, I'm here,' came her voice from his shoulder's left.

There she was, but gone were the smiles that had skipped off with her through the darkness. Her hair was a nettle bush, her pink dress muddied and torn. She sat at the bottom of her cage, holding on to her pillars of captivity as it swung back and forth.

'Lily! What have they done, are you alright?' He searched the cage for a door, a release of any kind, but there was nothing but a tiny keyhole in its base. It sat just beneath that familiar golden plaque, reading *Lily*. 'What are you doing here?'

'I don't know, everything went black and suddenly I was in this cage,' she replied, kneeling up to meet his face. 'Listen, you've got to get me out of here. There's skeletons and there's creeps and... and... the rocking of the train is making me feel quite sick.'

'There must be a latch or something,' Vincent replied, running around the hanging cell. He stopped after a single rotation and brought his face close to hers. 'Are you truly real?'

'Of course I am,' she said, holding his hand in her own. Familiar but cold.

He pulled his hand away almost without thinking.

'Why did you leave, Lily? Why did you run and leave me all alone?' He felt the rage boiling, the froth rising up his sides. 'I could have helped you and instead you left me in the dark!'

'I'm sorry, Vincent, it wasn't a choice,' she said, tears falling like curtains. She pulled her own hands away too, cradling them to her chest as if her glass heart might shatter. 'One moment I was there, the next it was all blackness and then I was being thrown in this cage by a man with arms like buffalos! If I could have stayed I would have, you know I would!'

'You're supposed to be coming to my party! You promised you'd be there!'

'Oh, so this is my fault? I obviously *chose* the party in the sky over your own, I *chose* to tread the path of the dead rather than go to that bloody school one more time. Silly me, for not tearing up Death's invitation the moment it slipped through my letterbox!'

She rushed back to the bars, a pleading in her eyes.

'Get me out of this blasted place, Vincent. Find a way to set me free and *bring me home*.'

Vincent searched the cage like a squirrel looking for a forgotten nut. Nothing new of note.

'Well, is there a key anywhere?' he asked. 'Where there's a lock there must be a key.'

Lily scratched her chin as if she'd become male, and eighty.

'The man with buffalo arms!' she exclaimed. 'He had keys. Used one on this very cage after throwing me in, if I remember right. A whole bustling ring he had, keys all jostling amongst themselves.'

Buffalo arms.

'Oh, you must mean the Conductor,' said Vincent. The man's arms had been enormous. Covered in a thick pelt, too. 'Did he have a face like a pirate cove?'

'That's the one! Like the faces of Mount Rushmore, having taken a few punches. With a meteorite.'

'Brilliant. Where can I find him?'

'Conductor's cabin, I would have thought.'

'Yes, but where's that?'

'Front of the train. Usually is.'

'Thanks. You've been a great help,' he said, each word dripping with sarcasm. The smallest of smiles broke the tension on his face, but quickly melted like thin snow. 'I'll be back as soon as I can,' he added.

'Oh, no rush. I'll just be here, trying to block out the screams.'

Vincent turned towards the front of the train, towards the roaring smoke.

'Vincent?' came a sweet voice from behind. He looked back.

'Try to be safe,' she said. 'Last thing we need is both of us trapped in a cage.'

CHAPTER NINETEEN

An orb of blue and green, spinning through nothing, just one of many yet so alone. Swirling down the drain of a pool of black, so full of life and, as such, so full of death. A gaunt figure watched it turn, ambivalent to its concerns.

There had been a beginning, of that the figure was sure, and everything that has a beginning must have an end. Everything grows cold eventually. It might take a few trillion, trillion years, but the figure of white could wait. He had Time, after all.

His fingers tapped against the window, through which he watched it all. It echoed hollow. He watched it start; he watched it finish. The universe was quite happy to end. Those made of flesh and dreams, they didn't seem to care for the idea quite so much.

There had once been a day without a yesterday. There would be a day without a tomorrow. And it was the same for each one of them that walked the streets and lay in their beds; they each had a day without a yesterday, and they would each have a day with no tomorrow. Time trickled away, and he waited for each and every one of them.

The figure sighed.

What are man and woman but flecks of dust; a fleeting mote adrift with barely a place in space nor time. Divining purpose where there is none. What are man and woman but shapes of chance, a way for matter to congratulate itself — oh well done, indeed — and deny inside the truth that everything is deeply, inherently empty. An endless, hollow void through which they spin in ignorance, standing proud in what they boast as form.

Day after day the glorified petri dish waltzed its way through the cosmos, and day after day he watched as numbers grew and numbers fell. Nothing cared in the slightest, except the numbers themselves. They seemed to think it was important.

Bless them.

Another tap on the window, another hollow echo. The vision swirled and then came back into focus. Two pits as deep as eternity bore down, and out of this black the Pale One watched.

* * *

Harrington Primary School continued on in Vincent's absence, just as it had with Lily's. The only change was that two seats sat empty rather than one. Well, a third was bare but that was for an entirely different reason; Billy Bradshaw's parents had deemed a family holiday during term time to be more important than their son's education and future prospects. They weren't too smart themselves.

Children scribbled essays. Homework was handed in on time. Laughter still pierced the cloudless sky of the playground, only now from the playing field too.

Babies were born. The elderly died. More babies were born than elderly died. The planet kept turning, and the human race kept trying to survive.

Anna sat at her table and stared across at the missing diner. The room felt all the more empty without his innocent smile, or even the irritating scratching of his fork as he pushed his greens around his plate. And now she did the same, the shrill dragging of her cutlery cutting through the torturous silence. Time was towing a heavy weight. The house felt too big.

The neighbours continued to tend to their gardens, mowing the lawn and watering the flowers. Those flowers continued to grow. So did the weeds. The local boy kept peddling his bike as he went about his paper round. Cars continued to drift by the window like seagulls in the seaside air.

Some of those cars went to the supermarket. Their passengers walked up and down the aisles, shovelling plastic meat into their trolleys. Being coerced into buying deals for products they neither want or need. Wafted with the aroma of freshly baked bread. Buying the latest film, and looking forward to watching it with the family that evening.

Grandma sat in front of the television, though the screen lay black and bare. Her needles went *clack, clack, clack*, and wool took its time and shape. She worried for her grandson; she worried for her daughter; she worried, and felt guilty for her selfishness, that her family line had come to an end.

People worried, and people rejoiced. Most just simply lived. Many died and many more mourned, but the world did not bat an eyelid.

* * *

Vincent never thought he was all that special. He wasn't bad at running - the couple of Sports Day relay race near-wins had brought that to light - but no, he never considered himself particularly special. Lily though, now he had always thought her special in some way. And not just because she was different - far from it. Because to him she was just like anyone else, and like anyone else she was special.

Obviously, he was wrong.

It's easy to fall into the trap of thinking that oneself is special or, if oneself is too depressed and self-deprecating, to believe that everybody else is instead. It simply isn't true.

Nobody is special, or at least, nobody is special simply for existing, which people seem to think is special enough.

Vincent loved the sciences, particularly when it involved space. The universe was huge, he knew that, and the Earth but a tiny blue speck. He was just one boy amongst billions, sitting on that speck.

Some consider it lucky that the universe is ruled by physics that allow for matter to form. Vincent certainly knew it was lucky that the Earth was at a certain distance from the sun - not too cold that nothing could grow and not too hot that the atmosphere boiled away into space. Like many he thought it lucky that life had chanced at all, and that excited molecules had chosen to join together for complex life. He felt lucky that mammals formed, and apes emerged, and men grew from apes. He would have considered it lucky that environmental factors had encouraged homo sapiens' brains to grow, and to drive all other humanoids to extinction, had that been deemed appropriate for a ten-year old's syllabus. He certainly thought it was lucky that the chain of life from him all the way back to the first humans, and all the way back to the apes and the mammals and the fish, and the cells before that, had remained unbroken.

Vincent felt very lucky, and he felt that this fact made everybody quite special indeed.

Again, Vincent was wrong.

In a sea of infinite universes, there are infinite that allow for life to form. In each that do, uncountable billions of stars dance with planets in just the right position to do so. And all it takes is for one, *just one*, of those billions of planets to have excitable molecules, to have the right conditions for brains to develop, to get all big and wrinkly, and hey presto: the universe looks back at itself with a sense of wonder.

It's not luck. It's inevitability.

The only way for Vincent, or his mother, or his grandmother, or any of the shoppers in the supermarket to look back at their family line in wonder, is for their family line to have remained unbroken. If theirs had ended, and somebody else's had continued, then it would be them looking back, admiring how special they are instead. There's got to be somebody looking back, otherwise there'd be nobody to think themselves special at all.

One planet, somewhere in the entire multiverse, would inevitably harbour life. And that life would consider itself special, simply because it had the means to do so. It's a very human thing, to take such a self-centred view of one's species and its value. It's a very human thing, to create a sense of being special to disguise the fact that, outside of our inevitable, tiny, blue speck in a sea of black, we all mean nothing at all.

CHAPTER TWENTY

Vincent crept down the corridor, trying to carry his entire weight above himself so as to not allow the carpet to commit a single creak. Gone was the whipping of the wind and the judging stare of the sun; here the light came from bare, flickering bulbs.

He walked uninvited amongst the silence, through a passageway that looked more like a 1920s art deco hallway than it did the interior of a howling locomotive. Much like the passenger cabins the walls were soundproofed, like a toddler scrunching up his eyes and sticking fingers in his ears. See no evil, hear no evil, and all that.

And yet Vincent couldn't help but feel a thousand eyes watch him, follow his every movement. He wasn't supposed to be here, and he felt the threat of being caught as a very real weight upon his shoulders. A weight that made walking without creaks a pretty delicate task. Were those cameras hidden amongst the shadows of corners? Did curious eyes watch from through the spy-holes of doors to either side of him?

He pressed on with the tips of his toes. He felt like the character in his 'Agent Thompson' spy books, sneaking through bunkers and stealing secrets. The longer he walked the more he felt watched, but also the more he felt nobody else was there. Hopefully no henchmen sporting tommy guns, at least.

Left, right, left; still the corridor snaked with twists and turns.

And yet, somewhere far ahead, Vincent could make out the final, ultimate ticks of a clock, each landing with the crack of a thrashing whip. The sound grew closer, swimming through the halls like Captain Hook's crocodile.

Vincent turned one last corner and found himself blocked by an enormous clock, face to face. The pillars of Roman numerals stood a foot high; the more slender of the hands rotating like a gentleman's walking cane. But it didn't turn clockwise, rather it ran counter, and threw each second aside.

Looking back, Vincent saw nothing but empty corridor. This was it - the end of the line. He studied the timekeeper's edge and sure enough he found a hinge; this was a door no different than those huge hatches in bank vaults, portals to gold bars and mountains of paper notes. No metal wheel stood in its centre though, and no iron bar stuck out for it to be pulled open either. It stood locked. Each second that slipped by, every violent turn of the hand, was chased by the anxious panic of his heartbeat.

His eyes canvassed the clock, looking for a clue of any kind. He found one, etched across the minute hand in cursive, golden leaf.

'To pull aside this cabin door, the larger hand must come before,' he read aloud.

A riddle! Vincent liked riddles. This seemed a little more tricky than the ones on the back of his cereal packets, but he'd be damned if he wasn't going to give it his all just the same.

The larger hand must come before. Must come before what?

The hour hand was a fraction over twelve. The minute hand rested on two minutes past the hour. That of the second was rushing all too quickly past the twelve and eagerly towards the eleven.

Sweet walnuts and mullwaffles, only two minutes left on the clock.

Vincent didn't know what would happen when the minute hand hit twelve, but something deep in his imagination strongly suggested that he not find out.

His mind raced. *To pull aside this cabin door, the larger hand must come before.*

One hundred seconds left.

Okay, forget the first part; to pull aside this cabin door doesn't say anything, does it?

Ninety seconds.

The larger hand must come before. Come before the door pulls open?

He pulled at the minute hand, hoping it might give towards him like a secret handle. It remained vigilantly between the first and second minute mark. Another tug to be sure, and then he had to let go quickly before the second hand crushed his fingers as it passed.

Sixty seconds left. Half the time had gone and all Vincent had achieved was a louder pounding of blood in his ears.

C'mon, Vincent, think. The larger hand must come before. Come before. Before.

Forty five seconds.

He looked at the numbers around the edge, all I, X and V. They swam amongst one another, spilling and falling.

Thirty seconds.

IV.

Twenty five.

Before. Be fore. Be four.

Twenty seconds.

To pull aside this cabin door, the larger hand must come be four.

Fifteen.

He grabbed the minute hand with both of his own and pulled it to the right as hard as he could. It resisted like a rusted handbrake but sure enough it gave in, clicking through each minute with the stubborn resistance of bicycle gears. The second hand went in for the kill, crushing his fingers as it passed. Vincent screamed though he tried to trap it within, but still he did not let go. He pulled the hand down as the second passed beneath, scraping the skin from off his knuckles.

Three, two...

The minute hand clicked into place against the number four.

Silence. That meant that the clock had stopped ticking, at least. But for good or bad, nothing seemed to have happened.

Then, just as he pulled his raw fingers free, he heard the tiniest click.

The tiniest sigh as air peered out from around the clock face's edge.

Vincent pulled at the hands, and this time felt the doorway swing open. It was heavy, but seemed to swing readily on its own momentum. A circular hole stood in its stead, two feet deep.

Careful to maintain the new level of hush, Vincent crept inside.

This was the driver's cabin, alright. It was all archaic computer machinery and levers, bleeping lights and dangling chains. Stretched across the front were four glass windows, and through them shone in slanted squares the harsh and desert sun. Scuttling beasts ran across flat, yellow plains as the train stormed across the tracks.

A man lay crumpled in the driver's seat, face pressed against the console. His rail conductor's uniform was falling away in tatters, his eyes staring blankly across the room. The flesh was retreating from his face, and his teeth broke through in a desperate smile. One hand, half skeletal, had jammed the main lever forward, pushing the train ever onwards, faster and faster along its path.

Even in death, the driver managed to be less late than a Southern Rail service.

Vincent dreaded walking any closer to the corpse, but luckily a noise like a rutting pig approached from his right. He was glad to be mistaken; the Conductor sat in a fold-up metal chair, his head slumped forwards, snores rumbling from his mouth like sows off a production line. If he hadn't resembled an avalanche in clothing, he could have looked almost peaceful.

Dangling from his belt were the keys, a jailer's symphony of silver stalactites. Occasionally they'd knock against one another like shrill wind chimes along to the rise and fall of the Conductor's chest.

Vincent had no idea which key would work on Lily's cage. He'd have to take the whole lot.

He stepped forwards and felt the metal floor shake under his weight. Amongst the silence it was like a tin can being rattled on the end of a stick. Icicles crept over Vincent's spine, melted only by how deep the Conductor's sleep seemed to be.

He edged forwards like a house cat stalking a field mouse - feeling more confident than it really should. If the man woke up he'd be in *big* trouble. Either one of those arms could snap him like a twiglet.

Every second made Vincent feel as if he was balancing atop a mile-high podium, knowing that the fall would come sooner or later. It only needed the slightest imbalance.

A blast rang out, a bass-tone horn. Vincent's head tried to go in two directions at once - to look at the source of the noise and also the enormous man surely awoken from his slumber. His neck ached. The aural intrusion appeared to have come from a steam vent, in much the same way as a fog horn would sound out from a ship. Its chimney lid had flapped open like a cawing bird, screaming across the desert. It was as if some malicious orchestra member had put Vincent's head inside a tuba to wake him up.

And yet it seemed to have no effect on the Conductor. He sniffed, rearranged himself in his chair and folded his arms, but otherwise remained asleep.

Slowly Vincent's eyes returned to their normal size. He'd half expected to see the corpse standing up from the console, pulling on the chain that led to the train's horn, grinning with pride and success in foiling Vincent's plan, but there he sat, grinning in blissful ignorance.

Vincent reached down and gave the keychain the slightest tug. It pulled on the Conductor's belt loop but the man didn't respond. He was in a dream more deep than one of Grandma's naps. Good. He eased the clip open and slipped it free, holding it at arms length like a scientist with plutonium. So delicate was his payload, and so nervous were his hands.

He tried to cram the keys into his pocket as silently as possible. It sounded like sleigh bells fighting a cutlery drawer.

And then, when he could suffer the tension nor the excitement of freeing Lily no longer, he ran.

CHAPTER TWENTY-ONE

So many keys, no clue as to which went where. Big and silver, small and bronze, ones that looked like pins and others as twisted as horned devil's fingers. Three dozen or more spun and swung in Vincent's hands as he sprinted across the roof of the train, the buzzing of the wind dancing with the jangling of metal.

He could smell the red hot excitement, taste it as it pooled up in the back of his throat. His jackhammering heart throttled his lungs, so only bursts of breath slipped out. He was so close; *she* was so close. A slip of a key and they'd both be home free. Opening that cage was their ticket out of this place.

He just needed to work out which key.

'What does a cage key even look like?' he asked himself from underneath the screaming steam.

He felt the wind whipping at his back, delivering lash after delicate lash. His t-shirt flapped around his chest like curtains in a storm. He was thrown by the current, riding its wave, driven faster than his legs would ever allow on their own. Driven by a hope he would never forget.

He reached the cages, and blocked out the sight of emaciated bodies and their screams that filled the air. Hungry fingers plucked at his hair as he passed, but he cared little. The pleas of shrunken women and bawling babies were carried far from his ears by the gale, and all he saw was the path back to Lily. All other cages grew grey, then black.

He didn't think. He just followed the trail through instinct, darting with all the intent of a heat-seeking missile. He stumbled, grazed his knee on the metal floor, but carried on without so much as a pause. Sunshine was raining down, and no storm would blot out that sky today.

He reached her cage, his heart doing a tap-dance upon his ribcage at the sight of her bright, optimistic smile. She sprung to the bars.

'Vincent!' she cried. 'Did you get the keys?'

He dangled them in front of her face like he would to a cat. They jingled.

She raised one eyebrow in response.

'And which one opens the cage?' she asked.

'Ah,' he replied. There suddenly seemed to be a lot of cages all around them; what if her key belonged to a whole other ring? What if the Conductor was on his way back up to the roof, with a fire in his heart as angry as the furnaces in the train's? Excitement easily melted into panic without much of a bridge between.

He tried to match up the keys to the lock at the base of her cage. The problem was they all looked as if they could fit. He'd have to go through them, one by one. He suddenly noticed his hands were shaking, but couldn't tell which emotion was tugging at them.

He grabbed at the first key on the ring, long and silver with two blunt teeth. It went halfway through the lock, but wouldn't budge any further. The second, a stunted bronze number with a head like a jigsaw piece, fared no better. When the eighth failed to make an impression, Vincent's hope was close to death. By the look on Lily's face, her's wasn't long for the world either.

'Don't worry, Lily,' he said, flashing her the briefest of sad smiles. 'This was the only keyring on the Conductor; it's got to be on here somewhere.'

'Yeah, of course,' she said, but he could read the shades of blue crossing her eyes. 'Probably be the next one you try!'

It wasn't the next one he tried. Or the one after that.

Eventually he came to a key that felt frail and cheap compared to all the rest, a small, wooden piece carved from knotted grain and chipped from use. It dangled by just a thread of wiry string, apart from all the rest. It seemed at odds with the metal lock of the cages, but Vincent knew this would be the one. It was different, just like Lily. It *had* to be the one. It just had to be.

'Hurry, Vincent,' Lily whispered, breaking him out of his spell.

He felt the cold wood between forefinger and thumb, and traced the rise and fall of the grain. He put it to the lock and felt the teeth punch each tumbler up, one after the other. It hit the end. It fit.

He turned it to the left and...

'Stop there, boy.'

A hand as heavy as a mountain fell onto his shoulder. He could feel his bones creak and grind beneath. He looked up at a face like a giant's pebble driveway, bathed in shadow.

'Can't let you do that, boy,' he said in a deep rasp.

'I'm s-sorry, sir,' spluttered Vincent, looking back at Lily's frightened face. She had cowered at the back of her cage, her knees tucked under her chin. 'I didn't mean to steal, I, I-'

The Conductor took Vincent's hand away from the key, which lay still in the lock. His grasp was gentle, but firm.

'Oh, it's not that. It's not that at all, son. It's not the stealing that's the problem. It's just that our King,' - and with that word Vincent saw the man's eyes turn from brown to a glistening red - 'can't have you just rocking up to his front door as if *invited*. He's got a reputation to keep. It's never that easy.'

He picked Vincent up, one hand under each of his armpits. It was like picking up a baby - a baby made of feathers. Really light feathers.

'Put him down!' screamed Lily. 'Put him down!'

'Are- are you going to kill me?' whispered Vincent, nose-to-nose with the Conductor. 'Please don't, I'm sorry, I shouldn't steal *I'm sorry-*'

'Save your sorries, son,' said the Conductor. 'You won't be dying, not by my hands. No, the Dark One needs you around for a little while longer. He just needs you around *elsewhere.*'

And with that the Conductor threw Vincent from the train. The wind whistled in his ears, the world turned upside down and the distant, shrill scream of *Noooooo* flipped back and forth from behind.

Round and round like a barrel he rolled, and far through the air he fell.

CHAPTER TWENTY-TWO

Two days.

That's how long he'd been under - two days. It was so alien, so unnatural, so wrong for him to just lie there, motionless, save for the patient breathing and fluttering of eyelids. She couldn't even begin to imagine what dreams Vincent might be having, what nightmares he might be trapped within.

Anna had returned home the previous night, upon the doctors' request, but it hadn't done her any good. Unlike Vincent she found sleep a distant stranger, though her door was open and welcoming. What she would do just to fall away, to escape from reality for only a moment. Now she sat at his bedside, eyes swollen and red, head throbbing and dizzy.

Is he dreaming of me? Is he hungry? Is he in pain?

He could be screaming under there. Hammers could be driving nails into his extremities for all she knew, and there was nothing to do but sit and wait. She may as well wait for an eternity.

It had taken long enough to get over it last time. Three years. *Three years.* She couldn't go through that again. For so long there'd been a shadow where he should have been, lying in bed beside her, sitting across from her at the kitchen table. An empty, silent echo, reverberating through the walls of their house and hovering so heavy in each morning drive to the school. Three years to come to terms, and another seven still feeling as if a part of her was missing.

She'd never loved anyone as much as she did Vincent, but Robert came close. Their marriage had followed a whirlwind romance, but she'd never regretted a moment. It was as she'd always wanted, and when her belly grew four years later, everything had been perfect. Nearly. When Vincent came into the world, *then* everything had been perfect.

Then one morning, about a month or so after Vincent was born, Robert woke up, ate his cereal - little milk, so all the more crunchy - sipped his morning coffee, kissed them both goodbye and went to work. He climbed into his car, and then he was gone. He worked as a foreman at the local Wakeland Construction site, helping the latest block of affordable accommodation rise up from the earth. He had been walking across the site when a steel girder fell from a crane three storeys above. It crushed him, killing him instantly.

Three years. It was no secret that Vincent had been all that stood between her and the bottle or worse.

There came a rapping like that of a beak on glass at the door. Two faces peered in, tired and distant. They belonged to Mr and Mrs Bronte, Lily's parents.

'Rachael, David, sorry, come in,' said Anna, bringing her head up from hands still cupped like a beggar's.

'Sorry to intrude, we just thought we'd pop in and see how you both were.' Mrs Bronte's voice carried a hors d'oeuvre of pity and concern. 'We were just on our way back from town.'

'Picked up some new clothes for the summer,' said Mr Bronte, raising a large plastic shopping bag and a nervous smile. He sat down in the chair on the opposite side of the room.

'How are you feeling?' asked Mrs Bronte with a withering look.

Sigh. Here comes the entree.

'I'm fine, honestly,' Anna lied. 'Tired, mostly. Time seems to have taken on a strange sort of quality, the last couple days.'

'Yes, I'm sure it has. How's Vincent? Everything okay?'

'Oh yes, he's fine. Well, not fine, of course.' She ruffled her hands through her hair. 'He hasn't moved an inch. It's the waiting that's the worst, you know?'

'Mm,' replied Mrs Bronte as she made her way to the bed. Mr Bronte simply flashed a sympathetic smile. The crow's feet under his eyes looked as if they belonged to an ostrich.

Does she know? thought Anna. *Does she have any idea at all?*

She felt guilty all of a sudden, as if her grief was some selfish act. As if she wanted the attention. *Here are two parents having lost a daughter, and I'm sat mourning a boy still breathing. But is this worse, to wait and wait and never know the end? Was it a relief for them, when the closure finally came? What horrible questions for honest answers.*

And now the silence, marked only by the ticking clock and the awkward hum of lighting strips. So much to say and so much unspoken.

She didn't want to be alone but my God, did she want to be *left* alone.

And soon enough they were gone, grateful to be out from under the ominous storm cloud hanging over the hospital room and back under their own pattering shower, dissipating towards a clear sky. They'd been through so much, this must be but a prick of a finger compared to the limb they're surely missing. The thick weight of loneliness oozed into the room. She wasn't sure if it relaxed or drowned her.

Come on Vincent. Come back to me. Please, come back to me.

Yeah, she was drowning. Every breath was leaden, and her mind was adrift at sea without a sliver of land in sight.

There was something in the rocking of the waves that made her want to lie back, close her eyes, and just accept it. The worst that could happen was disappearing into the deep.

She brushed the hair back from Vincent's forehead and kissed him goodnight, for what it was worth. It seemed to be nighttime, at least. Maybe it was just the sickly lighting, but she could have sworn the shadows beneath his bed had become deep enough to fall into.

CHAPTER TWENTY-THREE

For the second time in Vincent's tale, his mouth was full of dirt. He spat and spat but grit dug in deep like sour soldiers in their trenches. The land of the dead lived up to its namesake.

At least *he* wasn't dead. Or more dead than he was before. Or something.

Still, he thought he'd keep his eyes shut for now. Keep the truth out that little bit longer.

When his eyelids broke past his begrudging defences and peeled aside, Vincent could just about make out the Rooma Express disappearing into the horizon. The tracks stretched back to him from infinity, spelling out a clear message: 'you missed your ride'. It was nothing more than a speck, made real only by the tower of smoke it offered to the heavens, mirrored by its ominous, stone counterpart. It was on its way to the Dark One's castle at a speed no Sports Day relay-race runner-up could compete with.

And with it went Lily, still caged. Vincent sighed; he was never going to get her back. It was hopeless.

He rolled onto his back and felt the sun tear down upon his face. It wasn't as pleasant as he'd hoped. He got to his feet, backed away from the tracks, and smelt burnt coal waiting in the air.

He would never catch up, and he was stuck here in the middle of the desert. Nothing but sand and stone as far as the eye could see, save for that ever-growing tower. Even in the small time he'd spent aboard the Rooma Express, the clouds circling the castle's spires had engulfed a great deal of the pure-blue sky, scaring the rest away. He guessed he had two options: stay here until he was nothing but a crisp, or use that time to walk the long road to the tower.

An ice-cold whisper of wind across his neck suggested Option Number Three had just become available.

Magnificent iron gates stood before him, held by an enormous archway ripped straight from one of Vincent's horror novels. In those they would have opened to haunted mansions and asylums, tied shut by the poison ivy snaking between their bars and spikes. Keeping monsters in more than their unsuspecting victims out. But these were different, and although he'd never seen them before in his life the way they stood open felt eerily familiar. As if they were welcoming him in.

Above the doors hung a sign, weathered and old. Cemetery, it read.

The way behind was still that hot, arid landscape. But where it had once stretched out endlessly ahead was now a cooling darkness, a calm and quiet night. The iron fence spun out both left and right, a clear and harsh divide, and over the threshold crept a white and milky mist.

'Is that him, then?'

A squawking, shrill voice rang out from above. Vincent looked up and saw three less than glamorous vultures perched atop the cemetery sign. One of them looked particularly fat and ravenous. Its tongue was lolling out.

'I should think so,' said one of the other birds. 'Though how he's gotten so far with those limbs is beyond me. He doesn't even have wings.'

Vincent found himself checking his arms as if his lack of wings might be something to defend. He snapped himself out of it.

'Excuse me, who do you think you are?'

'Vultures, of course. Can't you see?'

'Well, yes. But what do you want?'

'Oh nothing, not yet.'

The more distinguished of the three vultures slapped the fatter one with its wing. His saliva was dripping from his mouth like a broken pipe.

'Cut it out. It isn't time.'

'But he looks so delectable. I could just imagine a rack of his ribs with a big dollop of barbecue sauce…'

'Hey!' interrupted Vincent.

'…Or maybe just the legs, deep fried?'

'Stop it,' repeated the vulture in the centre, accompanied by another slap that almost knocked his drooling companion from off the sign. 'He's not on the menu. At least not until the Dark One has left him a lifeless husk. We are scavengers, after all.'

And with that the three vultures took off in the direction of the train and the tower beyond. Feathers fell from them like autumn leaves. Vincent could hear them arguing amongst themselves as they disappeared into the horizon.

So weird, thought Vincent. *So very, very weird.*

The train was so far ahead now, and the road so dry and long.

What the hell. I'm not going to catch it up that way anyway.

He stepped under the archway, and felt the graveyard's cold embrace the moment his foot left the sand. It felt like when his Mother went into the fridge and then put her hand under his shirt. He really wished he'd been granted a jumper when brought into this place. Each hand went under the opposite armpit, and he turned around to pine over the scorching heat.

Oh goddamn it.

Gone were the yellow plains, the blue skies and shimmering waves of swelter. Instead stood only a sea of black, so dark that Vincent couldn't tell, if he stuck out his hand, if he would feel a wall or lose it amongst lapping shadow.

Vincent conceded that he may have made a mistake.

He turned back around and was thankful - he thought - that his view to the front remained as he had left it. It wasn't particularly inviting, but at least it could boast consistency.

Shades of shadow in blacks and purples grazed across glistening lawns, their blades of grass twitching in the still wind. Branches, dead and black, wrapped in blankets of weeds and fallen from frames as skeletal as their neighbours downstairs. And all around, a hundred strong, lay graves of chipped, grey stone, each of them six feet apart and each of them alone.

'Just a creepy cemetery,' Vincent mumbled to himself. 'Nothing to worry myself about.'

With no way of turning back he hunched his shoulders and made his way down the cobbled path. Surely there was another way out of this place. At least it wasn't raining, though a tinge of apprehension in the air suggested a dramatic entrance wasn't far off.

Rotten leaves skipped across the path, dancing around the hollow echoes of his footsteps. His way was lit by moonlight, yet try as he might Vincent could make out no stars or sights in the sky. Pure, purple night had smothered the graveyard, broken only by the whispering, shivering breeze.

Little beads of light pushed forth from out of the graves; the grubs of Mother Spider's mountain poked free from the earth. *I haven't strayed too far from the path*, Vincent thought as the ghostly mist lapped at his ankles once more. The cracking of branches and the heavy flapping of wings came from the distant right, and he hurried his footsteps.

In time the path's cobbles became less regimented, dotted like spots on the earth. It was fading from beneath him, and soon it would vanish altogether. But just before it turned to mud and lawn, the path wound its way to an end.

Before Vincent stood a gravestone, small and white. It was new; it was clean; it was as plain as a stone can be. No flowers lay at its feet, and only one word was etched in bold upon its face. He leant in and peered through the darkness.

Vincent.

He groaned. So, that was it. He was dead. This was all some ridiculous fantasy created by the last dying synapses of his brain, an eternity preserved in an ever-present pocket of time. Well done religions of the world, you all got it marvellously wrong.

Wait, said a voice in his head. *If you're dead, then who the hell is underneath the ground?*

Ah, replied Vincent as lead anxiety turned to helium relief, *it's another cryptic message from my subconscious. As if I haven't had enough of those.*

Now that the grave didn't seem so horribly final it was merely horribly disconcerting.

'So one day I will die,' said Vincent to the empty cemetery. 'Tell me something I don't know.'

The cemetery replied with the kind of silence that's filled with very small goings-on.

'I'm aware that everything comes to an end eventually,' Vincent continued, throwing his hands to the air. 'It's just not something I need reminding of. And death is so far away, unless you're a hundred or something.'

Not for everyone, Vincent, came that familiar voice from within. *Sooner or later, you are going to die. You. Will. Be. Dead.*

Vincent shivered, but he didn't notice the cold anymore. It was true. One day he would die, just like everyone he would ever love would die, and there'd be nothing left but his decomposing body under six feet of dirt. A small piece of stone to remind those few that remained of where he lay.

And where he lay would be nothing - an eternity of nothing at all.

No matter what he did, this was where his story would end.

'So if that's where we all end up,' he said in a voice barely more than a whisper, 'what's the point of anything in between?'

A response came in the form of a harsh *caw* that cut through the thin air like a scythe through wheat. A crow stood perched upon a nearby cross, feathers as black as onyx. Through murderous eyes it looked down upon the boy, and from its beak hung a gold and brilliant lantern.

'Well hello, birdie,' said Vincent, the gravestone now forgotten. 'What are you doing, hanging around in a place like this? Looking for grubs?' he added.

The crow cocked its head and gave him a hungry look. Then it raised its right wing and shouted, 'Caw'.

'Yes, that is your wing.'

The crow rolled its eyes the best it could, given their static nature. 'Caw,' it repeated, and held up its wing again. The lantern swung, spraying the graveyard with a shimmering honey.

'Oh, you want me to follow?' asked Vincent.

'Caw,' replied the crow, and took off to perch on another headstone a little further on from his own. The ground below was muddy, with only patches of grass bursting forth as sporadic as the moss that crawled over the graves. The trees in spindly shadow reminded Vincent of the Dark One just before he had dragged Lily down into the depths.

He followed the bird as it alternated between hopping along the ground and fluttering through the air. Each time it would get too far ahead it would wait, impatiently, for Vincent to reach its light like a rower towards a lighthouse's beacon. Perhaps less of a lighthouse, and more like a siren on the rocks. Grave stones rose from the earth like row upon row of jagged shark teeth, as far as he could make out amongst the darkness.

He was sure he passed one that read 'Mrs Whiskers', his old cat that had died the year before. The image of a paw was emblazoned under her name, like a hand print along Hollywood Boulevard. And a little further up stood a tiny tablet, no greater than a shoe in size, with 'Bubbles' in miniature etching. A goldfish from so long ago it had almost been flushed from memory.

On and on he followed, twisting left and right whenever the crow alternated its path. He passed towering crosses, overgrown pillars and rusted plaques. His skin crawled whenever he crossed a mound of raised earth, or when he could make out worms wriggling underfoot. Sometimes not wriggling, when that foot lifted back up.

Then finally the crow came to a stop, flapping down upon a pristine headstone of dazzling white. It dropped the lantern to the side and let out one final *caw,* before tucking its head under its wing. Vincent approached with tentative footsteps, for he thought he knew which name would be engraved. He was right.

'It doesn't make it real,' he said to himself. The crow shifted uncomfortably. 'A grave for her is no more real than a grave for me.'

But in his heart of hearts he knew differently; he knew exactly what it meant. Lily had gone the way of Bubbles and Mrs Whiskers, and this grave was as real as any back home. She was but a ghost, yet only now could Vincent see her clearly.

He dropped to his knees and let the rain start to fall.

CHAPTER TWENTY-FOUR

The groundskeeper walked across the graveyard, his toes tapping a hollow rhythm across the cobbles. Every now and then they screeched like chalk being dragged across a blackboard. He was getting on a bit but he refused to believe he was any less agile than before. After all, everyone would be in a lot of trouble if he stopped making his rounds.

He would have raked the leaves, but there didn't seem much point. They'd only come spilling over the lawn again.

Clack. Click. Clack.

'Where is that damn bird?' he asked himself in tones older than time. The wind sent his cloak billowing around him. It chilled him to the bone, which wasn't particularly hard given his delicate frame. His teeth would have chattered like a pneumatic drill, but he didn't really mind the cold.

It wasn't that he couldn't see without Carol's lantern - quite the opposite. He saw everything crystal clear, day or night, in a high contrast black and white. He just missed the company.

He missed *familiar* company, that is. Somebody new had wandered into the cemetery, which was cause for concern. Most of its residents were not the wandering kind. So down that meandering path he followed, across cobbles and grass and muddied earth, to where the boy sat weeping at a headstone.

'I don't know what people hope to achieve,' the groundskeeper said in tones no ear could hear, 'crying over something so inevitable. Sigh. It's hardly like it comes as a surprise to them.'

He'd never understand people. Such fleeting, fleshy bags of tears.

Still, this particular sack of skin wasn't going anywhere unless he intervened.

He'd better not snot on my robe.

'Excuse me,' he said in his most human voice.

* * *

'Excuse me,' came a voice like the pendulum of a grandfather clock. It ran into Vincent's ears like tar.

The crow unfolded its wing and looked up with what could be described - in so much as a beak can smile - as glee. Vincent sniffed in surprise, then looked around too.

Well, there seemed to be a face. It just didn't appear to have any of the usual features. You know, like eyes, a nose, mouth. Ears. Or lips.

He looked away for a second, then back again.

Nope, still no different.

Where eyes should have been were just empty voids through which one could fall for an eternity or longer. Where a mouth should have been was a static, toothy grin. And where a face should have lain was a gleaming, polished skull of pure, ivory white. Glorious cheekbones. All wrapped in a hooded, black cloak.

Vincent was scared less of the skeletal figure before him, and more by the fact that he didn't feel scared at all. Even with a scythe as long as it was sharp and the grin of a thousand serial killers, the person in the hood wasn't frightening. He was just... there.

Where there should have been fear, his head was filled with a thousand questions. The levee broke and the first one came flooding out.

'Where's all your skin?'

The skull looked back with what was supposed to be disbelief.

'Why do you have so bloody much of it?' the hooded figure replied suddenly, throwing his hands in the air. He walked around Vincent, rested his scythe against Lily's headstone and stuck out a bony, sleeved elbow. Carol the crow hopped on dutifully.

He looked back at Vincent.

'Really?' he asked. 'You're faced with Mot the Destroyer and "Where's all your skin?" is the only thing you have to say?'

'W-who are you?' stuttered Vincent, getting to his feet. 'And what do you destroy?'

'I have many names,' said the figure. 'The Hooded One, Thanatos, the Pale One. And actually I don't do all that much destroying anymore,' he added. 'I just use it for old times' sake. It looks good up in lights.'

Vincent was looking more like a living statue with every passing second.

'Just call me Mr Muerte,' the skeleton offered.

'Well, pleased to meet you, Mr Muerte,' whimpered Vincent, holding out his hand.

Mr Muerte left it outstretched.

'Believe me, you don't want to do that,' he said, a wink in his unblinking socket.

Vincent retracted his hand, then used it to wipe a fresh stream of tears away.

'Oh dear.' Mr Muerte shifted uneasily in his robe. 'Why are you crying, boy?'

'Because-' and again another big sniff - 'because of my friend. She died, sir.'

'Oh,' said Mr Muerte, craning his long frame around to look at the front of the headstone. He brought himself back up to his full height. 'But why are you crying?'

'Because it's sad! She's dead, you strange man!'

'Well, did you not know it was going to happen? You do know that it happens to everybody, right?'

'That doesn't mean it isn't sad! Have you no feelings at all?'

'Oh. No, not really. It wouldn't go well with the job, I wouldn't think.'

An awkward silence fell upon the grave yard, though it wasn't nearly as heavy as the skeletal figure's gaze.

'So you're the Grim Reaper, right?' asked Vincent, readying his next words like a battalion of soldiers taking aim.

'I try not to be! I mean, it's not as if I'm not smiling all the time. But I suppose from everyone else's perspective...'

'Then you killed Lily! You killed her and-'

'No.'

Mr Muerte held up a bony hand, then dropped all but two fingers.

'For one, I don't kill anybody. I just claim their souls. And two,' and here Mr Muerte took another look at the gravestone, 'I don't remember a Lily. Was she ill, perchance?'

Vincent nodded solemnly.

'Ah, well that explains it. My sisters, the Keres, take all clients based on war, pestilence, accidents and murder. I'm sure one of them handled it, and to the best of their ability I might add.'

'So what do you do, then?'

'Accounts and promotion, mostly.'

He picked up the scythe, and it made a hum like the rubbed rim of a wine glass as it cut through the air. Carol jumped down, scooped up the handle of the lantern in her beak and fluttered back up to circle overhead.

'Well, I've got work to do and I can't have you loitering. You're like a little snotty weed out here.'

He click clacked his way down a path to the left, which seemed to have assembled itself from cobbles and pebbles while they'd been speaking. The tapping of his scythe created a waltz-like beat. A few metres along Mr Muerte turned around and threw a blank stare Vincent's way.

'Are you coming?' he asked.

Vincent caught up quickly. He thought it better to follow Mr Muerte than be alone, though he didn't think he'd ever felt more lonely than in his company.

'How old are you, boy?'

'Ten, sir. Almost eleven.'

'Lost many people have you, boy?'

'No, sir.'

'Well I've seen millions come and go. Billions, actually. It's necessary. Imagine a world full of everyone that ever lived. You'd never get to the front of the queue at the Post Office.'

He looked at Vincent.

'What's that human phrase? Nothing's certain except death and taxes - that's the one. You like it?'

Vincent shrugged.

'Hmm. I don't understand you small people. Such curiosity yet so little knowledge. So odd and so... messy.'

Carol squawked and dived at a worm as it frantically tried to wriggle its way back into the earth. It was speared by her talons and brought up into the air for a mid-flight snack.

'So, how old was she?' continued Mr Muerte.

'Also ten, sir.'

'Is that much of an age?'

'No. It's nothing at all. I keep thinking about what the rest of her life would have been like, what-'

'It's a great age for a fox.'

'Sorry, what?'

'A fox would be ecstatic to reach ten. What a grand old fox that would be.'

'But she wasn't a fox, she was a person! She was supposed to come to my birthday party, and she was supposed to grow up and get a job and get married and, and...'

'Tell me, boy. Why do you focus so much on what could have gone on after, and so little on what has come before?'

Vincent fell silent.

'What?'

'Well, if we all lived to ten, would her life be seen as wasted? Or would we take comfort in all the joy she filled hers with? After all, from her perspective she lived through all of existence.'

He had a point. Vincent could see all these shimmering mirages ahead, disappearing beneath wave upon wave of glittering grains of sand. But for all those visions of the future he was letting the past slip through the cracks of his mind, running the risk of losing all the happy memories along with it. Ten years of life and smiles, washed away by the bitterness of a shattered dream. He shouldn't swap ten good years for any amount of fictitious ones.

'Memory is all you've got, boy. Don't tarnish it.'

The faintest embers of hope sparked up in Vincent's heart...

'Not that it matters,' Mr Muerte continued. 'You all die soon enough, memories are forgotten and eventually there'll be nothing left but an infinite coldness. Enjoy it while it lasts, I suppose.'

...and were quickly doused by a bucket of filthy rainwater.

'How can you be so... so... so detached?' Vincent replied.

Mr Muerte stopped in his tracks and looked into Vincent's eyes, bearing down with all the weight of Time's tombstone. In that moment there was nothing but a pearly white skull – eternal, inevitable Death.

'Because in my line of work, imagine how I'd feel if I weren't.'

He rummaged in his cloak and from his sleeve brought out a key ring, only unlike the clattering conglomerate of the Conductor's his housed but the one key – large, skeletal and with enough teeth to out-smile a crocodile. He clutched it between bony fingers and suddenly there was no more cobbled path before them, instead the insurmountable barred gates of a crypt, stone and grey. The crumbling skull of a desert bovine was carved above the gateway, and counterparts from various species, of various shapes and sizes, cascaded down the archways to either side.

Mr Muerte placed the key into the iron gate's lock as if he was threading a needle. Each door of the gate swung open as if on a clockwork mechanism, but without uttering so much as a squeak of a hinge. Beyond lay a warm, pulsating glow.

'Coming in, boy?' he asked, stretching an arm out ahead of himself in invitation. 'It's a lot warmer down there than it is out here, or so I'm told.'

Vincent looked at the path that snaked behind. He could follow it back to Lily's grave, if he wanted. It was only a short walk, really. He would sit there just for a moment. And then just a moment longer.

'Come on,' said Mr Muerte, interrupting Vincent's train of thought like a fat cow on its tracks. 'I can't have you loitering anyway. You'll wake up the neighbours.'

He ushered Vincent through the door like a housewife would shoo out a dog, proud of itself having rolled in the mud.

'Just don't touch anything. Your hands are sticky with curiosity.'

CHAPTER TWENTY-FIVE

'Would it be considered polite for me to offer you a drink?'

Mr Muerte held out a glass of red wine, as dark and thick as blood. After a momentary pause he swilled it, as if doing so would make it all the more enticing.

'I'm ten,' replied Vincent.

'Oh, I see.'

The wine glass remained at arm's length.

'So that's a no, then?'

The room certainly was warmer than it was outside; a fire crackled away in a fireplace torn straight from a Victorian mansion. There was even a sheath of pokers at its side, though Vincent suspected that the fire kept itself. This wasn't so much a home as it was the idea of one – an ideal shimmering on the periphery of reality. A grandfather clock ticked away in the corner; two plush, leather armchairs flanked a coffee table of deep oak; and bookshelves lined the walls. Apparently Mr Muerte was very well read. He also liked candles; every surface seemed speckled in flakes of melted wax.

It was all incredibly pleasant.

Mr Muerte drank the contents of the glass in one quick gulp then closed the lid on his drinks cabinet. It was built within an antique globe, of course. Part of Vincent wanted to ask if he had any cola in there, but he suspected not.

A small light protruding from the wall flashed orange, accompanied by a quiet beep. Mr Muerte swatted the noise away with a bony hand, and the light replied with another tiny noise.

'I wish that would stop,' he said, rubbing his head.

'What's it for?' Vincent asked.

'Oh, it goes off whenever somebody passes on. It's relentless, honestly.'

'Aren't you going to do anything about it?' Vincent imagined ghostly souls at a station, wondering why their train hadn't arrived.

'Of course not, that would be exhausting. So many people dying every second, I'd never get anything done. Anyway, it's hardly like me turning up is going to make their day any better. It certainly wouldn't improve mine.'

'That's so heartless!'

Mr Muerte tapped his chest, and through the robe came a hollow knocking sound.

'Exactly that,' he said with a chuckle as deep as the Mariana trench. 'What's there to be sentimental over? People are born, people live and then people die. It's the case with every single one of you and it always ends the same. Yet somehow you all find it a shock, as if it's some sort of surprise! Humans die in their hundreds by the minute, and not one of them is more a loss than the others. They're just dust falling back to the earth.'

'No. No! You can't say that. You can't say that about me, or Lily, or… or… or my Grandma! Everybody is special – we're different and unique and we're not just dust or dirt or whatever you think we become after we die.'

It was admittedly difficult to tell, but Mr Muerte definitely grinned that little bit more. He pottered over to a mirror at the other end of the room – toes clacking against the wooden floor, of course – like an old man ready to disclose some terrible secret or impart some ancient wisdom. It was gold in rim and the glass was as clear as the waters of the Five Flower Lake.

'Let me show you something,' he said, dragging a chalky finger around the mirror's edge. The reflection rippled like a pond hit with a pebble, then rapidly writhed back to its original, perfect sleekness. 'Let me show you all the sanctity of death. How unique everybody is, in their final moments.'

The glass spun into a vortex, a whirlpool breaking into colour. Figures were born from shapes and scenes were set as the image came to fruition. Vincent found his nose to be hovering just millimetres from its surface, peering like a voyeur through a neighbour's window.

At a scratched and metal table sat a man, his thinning hair tumbling over the back of his neck. His vest top hung loose and carried stains of age, yellowed and frayed. His y-fronts fared little better. His face was wrinkled before its time and a beaked nose hung over breath sour with booze.

The room was in the grip of both light and dark; shadow crept in from the corners to flank the pale gaze of a single fluorescent tube. It hummed a dull melody overhead to break the silence. Two companions sat at his table: a half empty bottle of beer and a fully loaded revolver. Half a dozen fallen soldiers lay scattered by his feet. Dirty plates climbed over each other in the sink.

Fifty-two. Ex-warehouse manager - he lost his job when he couldn't turn up to work without a half-bottle of Jack already swimming in his belly. Ex-father - his daughter had become estranged when he started turning up to meet her with more than a bottle in his veins. Ex-husband went without saying. He was alone, day-in day-out, and all his own doing. Yet he'd never had any control, and that would stop today.

He drained the second half of his beer. Yes, it would all stop today.

He picked up the gun and felt its weight sag in his hand. It was okay. Somebody would hear the shot and find him, but nobody would really notice. Nobody would *mourn.* And that was okay. At least he'd have stopped the cycle. This would be his choice, and his choice alone.

He put the gun into his mouth and pulled the trigger.

Vincent recoiled from the mirror as the blast rang out, but the image upon its surface was no longer that of the man in the vest. Instead it swirled into new shapes and colours, and once more Vincent's eyes were drawn closer and closer to the world beyond.

The sound of the gunshot twisted with it, morphing into a continuous wail. No – it wasn't a wail. It was a car's horn, ringing out like a siren to gawkers and rubberneckers alike. Drawing them to an accident that pieced itself together before him.

Two cars framed the picture, only the one to the right had the bonnet of a boxer's face. A very *person* shaped dent had found a home in its centre, in fact. The mould for this impression was currently lying about twenty feet away, for the most part. And here she had remained for the past five seconds, for she had very quickly realised there wasn't any getting up.

At least one of her legs was pointing the wrong way, which would have been enough trouble by itself. But none of her other limbs were any more cooperative. This would have been much more terrifying, were it not for the calming acceptance that washed over her senses. It was everyone *else* that seemed to be losing their minds.

The horn was still blaring, but she couldn't put a finger – or, she thought morbidly, any digit at the moment – on why it would be. Underneath the drone came first the screeching of rubber, then the opening and slamming of car doors. And then there had been lots of hurried footsteps.

That's about as far as things had got.

Her head felt hot. Actually, it felt hot and *wet*. That wasn't normal. Hmm. Was she bleeding? If only she could look and find out. She supposed it was the least of her problems anyway. She could see boots all around her, obscuring the beautiful coastline beyond. Their muffled voices did little to distract her.

Twenty-two. What an age to live; what an age to die. All those dreams, built over hope upon hope, and none of them worth a dime now. None of them flashing in front of her eyes, none of them desperately clawing for realisation as they shatter into a thousand pieces. Just the gentle lapping of the waves upon the coast, as a peaceful calmness mirrored its movements over her.

Ah well. None of it really mattered anyway – she could see that now.

One thing did concern her, however - a passing regret, slipping past in a stream of tranquillity. As colour turned to grey turned to black, she thought to herself: I really should have talked to my dad more.

At the end of it all, that seemed like all that mattered.

Vincent tore his face away, though his stomach went in directions all of its own. He bent over double as he tried – and failed – to keep everything inside. In the meantime, the mirror slunk back to its original state.

'Why would you show me that?' he shouted through sour chunks of subconscious.

Mr Muerte rushed over with the grace of a bat gliding in the night, as if not treading a single step, his cloak roaring behind like a comet's tail. Within a second he was practically on top of Vincent, encompassing all that there was around him.

'So you can see that everybody dies, all the time,' he said in leaden tones. 'Everywhere you go. Everywhere you look. Good or bad. Young or old. There's nothing special about it and there's nothing special about *them*.'

'No,' whispered a defeated Vincent. 'The chance of any one of us being who we are is astronomically small. That's what makes each of us so important.'

'Oh you ignorant child, still full of such human privilege. Don't you see that simply being alive isn't special in the slightest? You can only appreciate the odds of your existence *because* you exist. You're just one in a great many billions – inevitable, unspectacular and but a fleeting cameo in the course of history.'

He raised one hand to the air as if about to summon lightning.

'Perhaps it's time you got some perspective.'

His bony fingers clicked and time came tumbling in.

One, two, eight, twenty, four hundred, nay, millions, no, *billions* of sand timers rocketed past him, sitting stoic atop row upon row of shelves that stretched further up than even the heavens could aspire. They shot by like freight trains passing through a station, knocking him off balance and turning his hair into streamers. By the time they came to a sudden stop – as if they'd never moved at all – they stretched for miles in every direction; forwards, backwards and upwards.

A faint hissing of falling grains disguised itself as silence, falling with as deft a touch as the darkness spreading above.

'What are they?' asked Vincent, craning his neck to make out the vials hundreds of rows above. Vertigo sent him tipping backwards.

'The lives of everybody on the planet,' replied Mr Muerte, plodding down the aisle accompanied by the tapping of his scythe on the stone floor. 'There seem to be more here every time I visit,' he added resentfully.

Vincent stood in awe as he watched stream upon stream plummet in sandy waterfalls, spilling away the seconds of life in every human being on Earth. Each quiet moment was filled with such urgency, such finite finesse. Some timers were heavy with sand, others trickled away and others still lay as barren dunes, not a grain's movement to be seen. Each had a name in plaque upon its base.

'And when the sand runs out, they die?'

The grinning skull nodded solemnly.

'And that's when you come to collect them?'

'Allegorically speaking, yes.'

Vincent felt a burst of sudden inspiration.

'So you can reverse it, right? You could bring someone back?'

Mr Muerte shook his head and traced the rim of an hourglass with his finger. An old lady in Thailand, sweeping her floor, felt shivers run down her spine and gave a cursory glance over her shoulder.

'C'mon, Vincent. C'mon. It doesn't work that way. You know that.'

A hollow silence, smothered with grief, drizzled down.

'Where is it?' said Vincent.

'Where's what?' replied Mr Muerte, paying extreme attention to a particular hourglass in which he had little to no interest.

'Her hourglass. Lily's hourglass. Where is it?'

Mr Muerte tapped the glass distractedly. A small child in Minnesota experienced a heart palpitation.

'Three rows down, two aisles to the right. Middle of the second shelf.'

Vincent followed his directions to the letter, and what should have been a matter of seconds felt like the longest walk of his life. He knew that her timer would be no different from the gazillion other identical vials, yet bursting from his heart were visions of golden trimmings, of a timer much greater in size than any other. Perhaps he expected her casket; perhaps he hoped for a timer with sand still spilling away.

Three rows down, two aisles to the right, middle of the second shelf.

Lily, etched into the plaque. Normal hourglass. A small dune of sand sitting at the base of the jar, not a grain out of place. Utterly, perfectly still.

He reached out to it, but it was as uncomfortable as touching her actual cadaver. It was so, so cold.

Oh God, thought Vincent, *this is all so horribly hopeless.*

'What's the point?' he screamed at Mr Muerte, who had drifted silently up behind him. 'What is the bloody point? We're born for nothing, absolutely bloody *nothing*!'

He went to slam his fists against the ghostly figure but all they met were the swift, wooden blocks of Mr Muerte's scythe. It was like a bag of flannels being thrown one by one against the trunk of an oak tree.

'This isn't fair, it's not fair, why, why, *why*,' he cried, slumping into a kneeling position as his voice slowed like a wind-up doll running out of steam. It was a rather pathetic sight.

Vincent was yet to develop the agnostic approach to belief he would harbour later in life. It wasn't so much that at the present moment Vincent was religious, because he'd never really stopped to think about the details. It was simply that reality had yet to knock it out of him.

And so it was that Vincent started to pray.

'Oh bloody hell,' sighed Mr Muerte.

'Please God, bring Lily back to me, bring her back to her *family*, and see fit to rescue me from this dreadful place. Let...'

'There's nobody listening, boy.'

Vincent peeked out through a single eye, his hands still locked together.

'...what?'

'There's nobody listening. Hell, I don't know what's up there, or down there, or anywhere in between. I just do my job so nobody has reason to come down here complaining. But what I *do* know, what I know for sure, is that nobody is listening to a word you say. Not now, not to the words in your head, and certainly not just because your palms are slapped shut. And even if they are, do you really think they're going to change the rules for you? For one snivelling little boy?'

Vincent leapt to his feet and screamed. Mr Muerte would have been surprised, had he the capacity. Vincent grabbed the hourglass next to Lily's and, because he wanted it to be that of Lily's doctor, it was. He felt the immense, immortal weight of failure exude, the same weight that doubled as rage as he threw it down upon the cold, stone floor.

Where it should have shattered into a thousand fatal pieces.

It did not.

Dr. Paxter's hourglass sat back upon the shelf, no scratch or fracture to be seen, and all its sand still trickling away. It was as if it had never been moved.

So naturally, Vincent picked it up and threw it down even harder.

And naturally, it sat back upon the shelf again.

Vincent's anger was starting to wane, so he decided to change tack.

'Where's mine? Where is it? I'll swap hers for mine, you can have me, or I'll pour some of my sand into hers and we can share the time. I'll do whatever it takes, just show me where it is.'

Mr Muerte sighed. He was running out breath almost as fast as he was patience.

'That's not how it works, child. And no, I won't show you.'

'Why not?'

'Because you don't want to see it. Everybody thinks they do, and it's always a disappointment.'

Vincent's legs buckled out from under him, and he collapsed onto the floor once more. True enough, he didn't want to see if he had only minutes left to live. He felt so empty, as if somebody had come along and spooned out all his insides. Perhaps, under all that skin, he was just a wire frame like Mr Muerte.

Mr Muerte draped a blanket over Vincent's shoulders, having summoned it from the air. He was doing his best to be 'compassionate' and 'supportive', as he supposed the situation required it.

He'd try one last time to make this bag of crying flesh feel better, and then he'd give up.

'Look here,' he started. 'There's birth, and then there's death. Everything in between is just a waiting room. A waiting room for what, that's up to you. It really makes no difference. But there's nothing here: no purpose, no deeper meaning. You're born, you die, and most of you leave nothing more than a stain like a bug on a windscreen. This is limbo, and that's all there is.'

It didn't have the desired effect.

CHAPTER TWENTY-SIX

Jesus, if this took any longer he was going to kill himself. And then where would they be?

The Dark One looked up at the clouds circling and sighed. There was only so much patience he was prepared to summon, and right now it wasn't enough to fill a thimble. This was threatening to need an Olympic swimming pool worth of the stuff.

Lazy, lazy clouds, floating around as if there weren't any hurry. Was more misery required? Would that expedite the process perhaps? The Dark One rubbed his chin. It couldn't hurt, he supposed.

His tower was still growing closer to the stratosphere, now resembling the melodramatic dying reach of a soldier on the battlefield. It was really hamming it up. Any slower and The Dark One was pretty sure it would turn into a tunnel. And the clouds just kept swirling like water running down the drain. He wanted a vortex, something violent and fast. These clouds looked like those of a storm but they barely covered half the desert. How was he going to get through with half the kingdom still blazing like a tanning bed?

As the wind whipped around the roof of the tower, two familiar hooded figures came bumbling up to him. They bowed briefly before speaking.

'Sir, news from the kingdom,' said one of the Nightmare creatures, the one with more joints than he - or she - knew what to do with. 'Sir,' it added.

The Dark One sighed. Hell truly was other people.

'Yes, and what of it? I don't summon you here for the pleasantries.'

'The boy has reached the Pale One, sir,' said the other hooded figure, hovering forward as the other slunk away under shadow of cowardice. Its voice sounded like lead pipes and anvils. 'We have reason to believe he's suffering a bit of a breakdown at the sight of all the hourglasses. Sir.'

'Fantastic,' said the Dark One, clapping his hands together with such splendid gusto that Knees and Elbows went rolling over backwards. 'That should get the fires stoked, so to speak. And where there's fire, there's smoke...'

The hooded figures glanced at one another the best they could without discernible eyes.

'Do you want us to ready the prisoner, sir? We've prepped the equipment, and moved some of the tables around. Sir.'

'Yes, yes. Good.'

Soon, it would be soon. He could feel it running through him - the power growing. The boy would come, yes he would, and at the right time. No sooner, no later. And then it was just a matter of patience - yes, he hated waiting but it would be worth it - until the fracture opened and he could...

The Dark One was suddenly aware that there was no longer an absence of sound, rather the silence of two people trying not to make any noise at all. The two informants still stood behind him.

'Go, you fools,' he snapped, shooing them away with a backhand that a tennis pro would be proud of. 'If I wanted grotesque figures to gawp aimlessly then I'd install some gargoyles.' He gave the idea some serious thought as the two figures hurried down the stairs, still bowing and walking backwards. *It might brighten up the place*, he thought.

Where was he?

Ah yes. Soon. The boy would meander his way around Rooma, going in circle after circle, falling deeper and deeper, until all the boy's strength was lost. All the while he would be lapping it up, growing stronger. He grinned that smile of daggers at the thought of the clouds falling over the world, of everything turning to black and shadow. When all was smothered by its thunderhead blanket he would climb up, and cut his way through.

A whole other world, just waiting for Nightmares. Begging for it. Barely a fracture of reality away. What fun he could have! Billions from which he could leech, an entire planet for him to drain until nothing remained but a cold, grey ruin. And atop that ruin he would sit, surrounded by his legion, King of his Kingdom.

And such misery. He got shivers just thinking about it.

Bricks and blocks spiralled through the air around him like fat butterflies coming to roost, assembling themselves into the stonework that would carry him into the next world. The air crackled as lightning was released as fall-out. Frazzled oxygen stunk out the sky.

Far down below and even further away, the Dark One could make out a couple of figures walking amongst flowers. He tapped his fingers in idle thought. *Patience. A King must have patience.*

He turned and walked towards the staircase that spiralled through the centre of the tower. He needed to get a move on. Entertaining a guest could be a messy business.

CHAPTER TWENTY-SEVEN

Amongst the rivers of sinuous shadow and brimming black, the bed of lilies and posies shone like the whitest lighthouse beacon. A soft wind gave them strength to wave, interrupting a cacophony of wilted mourning.

Vincent had taken a little while to get over the hourglass incident. The blanket - which smelled of moth balls and past regrets, come to think of it - had helped a little. Mr Muerte's comments about everybody being a jumped-up bundle of atoms and dust incorrectly associating chance sentience with value and significance, not so much. A little, but not so much.

But eventually he'd come to terms with it. People die, and it's horrible. But it's inevitable, and people were just a blip in the lifeline of the 'big picture'. To the Universe, the time between the Earth being shaped and being engulfed by an expanding sun would be nothing more than a long weekend. He understood that, pragmatically, there wasn't really much point to anything, but he also knew that there was something far more personal that Mr Muerte, in all his bony, deadpan wisdom, was oblivious to.

It was on the tip of his tongue.

When he'd gathered the emotional resilience to use his legs for their intended purpose, he and the skeletal figure had left the hourglass cavern in hurried conversation. Distracted by near-infinite waterfalls of time, he'd forgotten that his survival and eventual escape from this place hung on a deadline. The irony.

It was imperative that he find a way back home, and soon. Mr Muerte had said that although helping the living wasn't strictly within his job description, nor really his skill set, he could lend a hand in reaching Vincent's destination. The way he said the last word sounded unsettlingly final.

So here he was, having travelled through crypt passage and torch-lit corridor, in the garden of death. Hugo Simberg would have been proud. No flower pots here though, just a sea of bowing, melancholy heads. Mr Muerte walked just ahead along the garden path, taking no time to admire the view. It was just another day like any other for him, Vincent supposed. They came across a gate, beyond which stretched an infinite field.

Apparently Mr Muerte knew a shortcut. It occurred to Vincent that an individual such as his Paleness probably wasn't constrained by such petty obstacles as time or space, but he thought it might be improper to expect more at this stage of their relationship. He didn't want to appear ungrateful, after all.

Still, unless he had a high-speed rail network running underneath the approaching meadow this particular cut didn't seem all that *short.*

Looming in the distance was a building, one that began small and grew into a large, wooden barn with every silent step they took. It was the single dot of braille in the page of silhouetted, swaying grass. The doors weren't locked or barred, and uttered a rotten yawn when opened. The inside was just like Vincent had imagined from the farms in the books he'd read years past, all wooden timbers, ladders and hay bales. His first thought was to dive into the latter from above, but given the pressing issues at hand it didn't seem appropriate. He couldn't imagine Mr Muerte approving, nor the single horse tethered at the far end.

In stark contrast to the warm browns and yellows of the barn, the horse stood in the striking black and white of the fields outside. Deep ebony were its eyes and hooves, while its luscious, spilling mane and muscular hide shared the complexion of its rider. No saddle straddled its back, but a familiar snort left no secrets as to who its master was. Mr Muerte scooped up some hay with his scythe and proceeded to feed it. It munched quite contently.

'Who's a good boy,' cooed Mr Muerte in what he could only have intended to be the voice of an old cat lady. It had the soft, soppy tones of a kitten being rolled over by a boulder.

'Who's a good boy?'

He turned to Vincent, sporting a definite contender for the award for most unsettling expression of the year. It was his usual face, or lack thereof, but simply more so.

'His name is Khloros. You can stroke him if you'd like,' he said. 'He doesn't bite.'

The horse looked at Vincent through eyes as old and uncaring as the stars. His hands made the executive decision to remain exactly where they were.

Mr Muerte patted Khloros twice on the neck before swinging himself up and onto the beast's back in one smooth movement. It was like a velvet shadow, fluttering in the sort of miniature tornado that only throws leaves around. One moment he was on the hay-strewn floor, the next sitting as gallant as a Queen's guard. The scythe hung murderously down by the horse's side.

'Hop on up, boy. There's nothing in this world quicker than Khloros, I assure you. Nothing *physical* at least. Rumours travel pretty fast, or so I hear.'

Vincent looked to his right and, as luck or some all-controlling part of his subconscious would have it, there stood a small step ladder. He climbed up and, after giving the horse a couple of pats of his own to ensure both its physical properties and reluctance to bolt out the door leaving him climbing up onto nothing but air, joined Mr

Muerte upon its back. Putting his arms around the skeletal figure seemed both inappropriate and ill-advised, despite the abundance of hand-holds his frame could provide, so he opted to pull on Khloros' mane instead.

'And yes, I would hold on tight,' said Mr Muerte, as if sensing the clammy nature of Vincent's hands.

He kicked against Khloros' side with one of his ossein feet, and from the moment of that collision everything became a blur. Khloros was quicker off the mark than any sports car - hell, any jet for that matter - and it only took a second for the comforting, glowing hues and freshly alarming aromas of the barn to be a thing of the past. The horse shot out through the open doors as if its hooves were rockets, galloping across the meadow at one, two, three hundred miles per hour. Each of its stomps pounded the earth with the ease of a palm through air. Then suddenly Vincent realised his hooves were doing exactly that.

At first it was difficult to tell, given a lack of features in the landscape to compare himself to. A sea of grass from two metres isn't all too different from a sea of grass from one hundred feet... so long as a sea of grass is all there is to see. But once something else enters the picture those blades of grass suddenly seem a long, long way down.

The desert, as harsh and familiar as the yellow eye of a favourite cat, rose up like an African predator. Its blinding sand was being swallowed by the shadow of enormous clouds overhead, but still he could see the perfect line of train tracks stapled across the landscape. He could make out the mound that was Mother Spider's home in the far distance. It radiated loneliness, but it was difficult to tell from so far away. Towering all around like the wall of a coliseum were the Big Ridge mountains; even from up here he couldn't see the world beyond. *If* there was a world beyond.

The air smelled thin and coppery that far up. Perhaps he was getting a nosebleed. He was certainly getting dizzy. He hadn't been this high before, not even at World of Fun. Or was it Thrill City? His stomach was doing somersaults, but it also seemed to be wearing a leotard stitched from lead. And that outfit was doing little to flatter his bladder, which desperately wanted to vacate its contents all over Khloros' back and send it spilling a hundred metres down like the world's longest waterfall.

'Look down below, boy,' said a voice from in front, unhindered by the wind rushing by. Sure enough, Vincent could see the Rooma Express chugging away along the tracks, steam and smoke rising from its various chimneys. And, dead or alive, Lily was still on board. Whether or not that even mattered anymore, Vincent wasn't so sure.

Up ahead from it was the tower, and once more he felt the bottom fall from his stomach and hang loose somewhere far below. He'd never seen it this close before, and with every moment that raced past it grew bigger and bigger and taller and taller. Its craggy surface broke and tore as it wrenched itself further into the sky, and with a sickening realisation Vincent knew: this was where the story would end.

He shut his eyes, knowing that that was exactly where Mr Muerte was taking him. For a dream, everything felt very *real*.

When Vincent finally opened his mouth to speak, and only after he'd gathered up the marbles of courage that were threatening to roll off the cliff of sanity, he found that the words came out as smooth and clear as if he was standing in front of his class, like when he'd given that presentation on what he wanted to be when he grew up. An astrologist, he'd said at the time. The wind buffeted the two riders, but their words hovered beside them in their own little bubble of audio.

He asked a question of which all men and women know, a question delivered with no regard for time, distance or reason. A question with only one, inevitable answer.

'Are we there yet?'

* * *

By the time they'd descended to the foot of the tower its spires had risen to but a point in the sky, a dot that the eye could only strain to see. The air was cold here, a world apart from the blistering breath of the desert, and tasted damp and stale. The stone, ever changing and burying into the ground like toes amongst a soft carpet, burst not from sand but from dry, brown grass.

'And here you are, boy. All change here,' said Mr Muerte, once Khloros had put hoof back to solid ground. Vincent had dropped the small distant to the floor and was now looking up at the hooded figure as he kept the restless beast from trotting around in any more circles. It didn't seem to like the onyx monstrosity any more than he suspected he would.

'Are you not coming with me?' asked Vincent, a little ashamed of how broken his voice emerged. He could see where the tracks of the Rooma Express led into the foot of the tower, but so wide was the tower's circumference that it would have taken a expedition team to reach it. There was no sign of the train either; it must have already reached its destination. This wasn't just the literal end of the line, he feared.

He could really do with an immortal, scythe-wielding sidekick right about now.

'Ah, 'fraid not, son. I've got souls to sow and books to keep, and all that.' He managed to get Khloros to at least point himself in the right direction, though not without some reluctant huffing. 'Though for better or worse, I'm sure I'll be seeing you soon enough.'

And with that he sped off into the night, or what served as good a purpose amongst the swirling dark clouds above. It only took a second for him to disappear from sight - a silver streak on a winter's night. Vincent looked up at the clouds and imagined he could see the twinkling of stars amongst the darkness, imagined that a billion burning souls gazed back at him. But that was just imagining, he knew.

He turned to the tower, with its walls so wide like the world's largest redwood tree, like the road bollard of the gods, and wondered how he would ever tackle something so insurmountable. He had literally no idea what he was doing. Literally no idea. He'd been swept along a surreal, distant current ever since Lily had died, whether in the real world or his imagination. Things were happening around him but he wasn't taking it in, as if his senses had been dulled and his reflexes cut. He felt as blunt as the stones that grew before him, lifeless and carried forward by an invisible force. He didn't know how he'd got to this blasted land. He'd been thrown onto a train. He couldn't say how he'd got to the graveyard and now he stood alone at the base of a monster's lair, a monster he was expected to slay in order to go home. To rescue Lily, and go home.

I'm a little boy, for God's sake. I'm not supposed to be fighting or slaying or doing any rescuing. I'm lost, thoroughly lost, and I'm supposed to do nothing but find a responsible adult and get a Tannoy announcement read out. Then my mum would come and take me home, and that would be the worst of it.

That wouldn't do though. Mother wasn't coming here. There was nobody here but him, and he would have to *Take Responsibility*.

Besides, it wasn't as if he could go any way but forwards. The path back hid land mines and bear traps beneath its roses and lilies.

Up fifty steps stood two oak doors, each tall enough for a diplodocus to march through. His calf muscles wanted to tear themselves apart by the time he'd reached the top. Nobody knows why architects design steps that are too wide and too tall to tackle comfortably with human legs, but they do. Two statues guarded either side of the summit, but like the tower they were yet to take final shape. Pebbles and grit spun in orbit around clumps of stone, taking form bit by gravelly bit.

Deep breath. This was it, no use in waiting.

He heaved against the wretched oak, and pushed his way into the tower.

CHAPTER TWENTY-EIGHT

Try as she might, Vincent's mother couldn't stop crying. Right now she was experiencing an endless stream of hiccupy sobs, the sort that emerge long after the well of tears has dried up.

'It'll be alright, Anna. I promise it'll be alright.'

The man holding her hand across the table had become a rock for her the last couple of nights. Hell, he'd even taken the day off and come to the hospital with her for support. She hadn't exactly been the best of company, but he'd stuck by her all the same. It wasn't how she'd imagined he and Vincent would meet, of course.

She'd been dating Chris for about five months, and it had been going well. Still was, in fact. Fantastically well, and that's what had always scared her. It wasn't that she had a problem with moving on - it had been a decade, after all - it was that she hadn't the slightest clue how Vincent would take it. He'd never really known his father, so perhaps he'd consider Chris a welcome addition to the family. But for all she knew Vincent could see it as a betrayal. It terrified her.

She'd been so scared to introduce them to each other. She'd known Vincent had begun to wonder why his mother was disappearing so many evenings, why he'd been spending so much time with his Grandma. And now he might not wake up, and they'd never meet... Oh it was helpless. Her thoughts were on a carousel, riding the horses up and down, round and around.

'Anna?'

She looked up into those deep, brown eyes. Those pleading, fatigued irises. He'd be here 'til the end, she knew that, but he needed her to come back to him.

'Sorry, yes. Yes. It'll be okay.'

'We just keep waiting, okay? Nobody has said that he won't wake up. If not tomorrow then the next day. You just need to stay strong.'

'But the doctors don't know what's wrong with him! How can they fix him if they don't know what's wrong?'

Chris left his chair and cradled Anna's head to his chest. He could feel the sobs struggling to break through every time she drew breath.

'I don't know, Anna. I don't know. But we need to try and stay positive.'

'This isn't right, I should be at the hospital with him...'

'And what good will running yourself into the ground do you or him? You need a rest. You need a break. You need to spend a night in an actual bed. We'll be back at the hospital tomorrow morning, I promise.'

Anna nodded. She knew Chris was right. After all, it was she who had suggested he come over after their hospital visit. She felt exhausted, but she couldn't bring herself to spend a night alone in the house. It seemed so terribly, terribly empty.

She moved the peas around her plate with her fork. They rolled like marbles, bombarding the sausages and ploughing into mashed potato. Chris' plate was empty, but she'd barely touched her dinner. Every time she brought the fork to her mouth she felt her stomach heave and her throat close up. She didn't really notice the hunger.

They got an early night, and though her partner made the shadowed silence of the house a little easier to bear she couldn't shake the feeling that something - somebody - was missing. Not just from the house, but from the world. Chris tried to comfort her but she couldn't return the affection. It wasn't that she didn't want to, exactly, rather that she had nothing to give. She felt as hollow as her home.

She did eventually fall asleep, but only after an age of tossing and turning. She kept imagining the hospital heart monitor going from beeps to a single monotone scream. She needed to be with him.

When she finally dreamed, she dreamed of spiders and shapes that should not be.

CHAPTER TWENTY-NINE

The great hall wasn't particularly resplendent, but the Dark One had made sure that a couple of crimson banners hung from the walls and a few candles were dotted around to brighten up the place. It wasn't really his style, but appearances are important when having people over.

They hadn't been able to do much about the mould though, nor the dark-green ooze that seeped in the corners.

A few hooded figures scuttled around in the background, doing their best to keep out of the way. Most used the floors, one opted for the ceiling. All were trying to appear as busy as possible, like employees the moment they find out Head Office is paying a visit.

The enormous doors creaked open with a laboured sigh; they knew it was their only moment in the narrative and were damn well hamming it up. A tiny shadow squeezed through the sliver of anaemic light before the doors dragged their way shut again. Silence was heralded by their leaden thump.

'Come to best me, have you boy?' came the Dark One's voice from the centre of the room.

Vincent walked forwards, feeling like a gatecrasher at the universe's most private, unappetising party. Everything was dank and poorly lit, though he had to admit the red drapes were a nice touch. A shadow took shape in the middle of the hall, bubbling into existence like the gaseous pops of a swamp. Road tar in the summer sun, dripping and scalding, only cold as the shivers that at that moment broke out across Vincent's body. He thought it would have been less scary if the creature had just lunged at him. Talking always made things more complicated.

'Well, actually,' Vincent said, thinking things over, 'I'd be quite happy just to go home and forget all about this vanquishing business, if it's all the same to you. Just show me the door and I'll let you get back to your…'

He looked around at the busying individuals watching him from afar.

'…interior decorating.'

That ought to do it, he thought. *Good job. Appeal to his sense of logic, he won't be expecting that.*

The Dark One seemed to contemplate this suggestion for a little while.

'Suit yourself.'

He wandered over to an area of the hall blanketed in a very full darkness, the type that serves only to mask its contents rather than that which pools through depth. Vincent simply stood there, somehow disappointed in how easy victory had been to grasp. So, like the foolish man that knows he hasn't *really* won that argument with his wife, he went back for more.

'Oi,' he shouted, pottering over alongside him. He wasn't sure what was worse: that the Dark One smell evil or foul or, as the case was, that he didn't smell of anything at all. He was as thin as a dream upon wakening, barely filling the space he occupied.

'Oi,' he repeated. 'How do I leave then? Why am I not home?' He considered punching the amorphous figure and thought better of it. 'And where's Lily, you creep?'

'It's only through necessity that I tolerate your existence, you snotty moron,' the Dark One sneered. 'I'd tread carefully and pray that I don't reconsider my options.'

He pointed at one of the many hooded figures trying their best to become the room's much needed furniture.

'You. Prepare the lights.'

He twitched a little at the sound of the final word.

One of the hooded creatures barrelled its way towards a wooden crank, and began pumping furiously with all three and a half of its limbs. The whirring of gears rose in pitch until they screamed a squeaky whine and then, one by one, the lights burst on like the popping of gunpowder.

First a leg. Then a lower limb. And then a leg.

From a massive frame of wooden scaffolding hung ropes and iron clamps, and from each of these stretched an enormous, hairy leg. Eight of them, in fact. Mother Spider hung in the centre like a giant, bristly gong.

'Well hello, dear,' she said when she saw Vincent below. 'I wouldn't stay around if I were you, I imagine things are going to get rather messy.'

She clacked her mandibles in the manner of someone tapping their fingernails upon a table.

'Though I'm guessing you haven't worked out how to get home yet. Never mind. It'll come to you.'

All of her many eyes swivelled towards the Dark One.

'If you could have that epiphany sooner rather than later, however, it would be much appreciated,' she added.

'Start the pulling,' said the Dark One, waving his long, willow fingers as if dismissing a waiter. A dozen figures snaked and galloped their way over to pull on pulleys and crank up cranks. Vincent was pretty sure he saw a tentacle slip out from where a face should have been.

'You might want to stand over there,' the Dark One added with a whispered hiss, nodding to a patch of stone a little further away. Vincent found himself complying.

'Heave,' screeched a servant with a voice like teeth against an angle grinder.

The enclave all pulled and cranked as hard as they could, a couple bouncing up and down on their pulleys like monks ringing bells. The ropes tightened and the iron clasps, fastened tight around each of Mother Spider's legs, wrenched tight like whips. She let out a guttural roar.

The Dark One held up one hand and everybody stopped. He approached Mother Spider's gigantic face and brought his own close.

'What I hate, is people getting involved in matters that don't involve them.'

He threw his hands up, exasperated.

'Was it too much to ask for the boy to walk across the desert? Did you have to give him a bloody train? Now I've got to deal with this dribbling meatbag myself! Do you know how slowly little boys walk through sand?'

Vincent felt like the friend of a child whose parents are arguing, who still expects to be invited to stay for dinner.

'No worry,' said the Dark One, relaxing. 'It matters not. Why fret over the journey when the end result's the same, aye? He needed to come here sooner or later.'

He patted the side of Mother Spider's suspended face.

'Still, would have been better had you kept your nose out of my business. Thank god we don't have a carpet.'

He beckoned to his many servants.

'Resume the pulling.'

The figures all sparked back to life, pulling or pushing whatever came to hand. The ropes creaked. The wooden scaffolding buckled and strained. Mother Spider screamed. And then she stopped, and closed her eyes.

With a terrible tearing noise her eight legs ripped from her body, first hanging by bone and tendrils then only scraps of flesh and hair. Gallons of blood rushed in waterfalls upon the floor, seeping through the cracks in stone, followed by the crash of her body. That sudden crescendo and then all was still, save the swinging of her legs from the beams above.

She lay as a bleeding ball upon the floor. Vincent didn't know what to say or do, but luckily the Dark One had it covered.

'Now I don't want you to feel that this whole mess was your responsibility,' he said, drifting over like a streamlined Nosferatu. 'She brought it upon herself and I'm to see no blame resting on your shoulders, am I understood?'

He spun around Vincent like dust in a vacuum cleaner.

'But what I need you to know,' he said, drawing close until Vincent could feel every word bite against his neck, 'is that everything from this moment on is your fault, and there's nothing you can do to stop me.

'You are nothing but a speck, an insignificant vessel through which I will be born into your world. Nothing more. You're here, and here you will stay, so that I can tear through, and all that follows, all the darkness that drowns you and everyone else you love in that silly little world of yours, all the shadows cast through sunlight, all the storm clouds that smother the last of the life you hold so very dear - that will be on you.'

The torso of Mother Spider twitched in an involuntary, posthumous viciousness for just a moment, though nobody paid much attention. The hooded figures had hurried back to the shadowy corners, hoping that the Dark One would pay them the same curtesy.

'Now who should I kill first, once I'm in your world?' he asked, draping his insectoid fingers across Vincent's cheek. 'Your mother? Or that wretched old grandmother of yours?'

'Don't you dare!' screamed Vincent, but try as he might his feet wouldn't budge. He waggled his arms for balance, which didn't exactly add weight to his threat.

'Ah, it matters not,' continued the Dark One as if to himself. 'When all is black and gone, know that it was I who took it from you.'

As if on cue the doors to the great hall opened once more, relishing another opportunity to steal the limelight. Cutting through their creaks came the steady knocking of wood on stone, like an old man hurrying with a cane. Vincent twisted his neck to see a cloth-clad figure fast approaching.

'Mr Muerte! Thank god you're here. The Dark One, he killed Mother Spider and he's...'

'Your Darkness,' nodded Mr Muerte, ignoring Vincent completely.

The Dark One grinned.

'Your Paleness,' he replied.

'I see the boy isn't giving you too much trouble. Looks like you're going to have quite the clean-up operation on your hands over there, though.'

'Well, if you're going to torture and dismember giant arachnids you have to accept a certain amount of spillage. My gratitude for delivering the child. He was put on an express train to me, of all things. An express train! This land exists for one purpose and it is *not* to expedite this little snot-factory's trip home. Absolute bloody nuisance.'

'Excuse me?' said Vincent.

'I mean, imagine him just turning up at my doorstep unannounced. "Hi, I've been here for three minutes and I'm ready to go home now." The cheek of it. That wouldn't...'

'I said, excuse me?' asked Vincent once more.

The two kings turned to face him.

'How come if you didn't want me turning up so early, you got Mr Muerte to bring me here?' he asked. 'Wouldn't it have made more sense to leave me wandering the desert?'

Mr Muerte looked as shifty as it was possible without eyebrows. 'You'd keep quiet if you knew what was good for you, boy,' he said.

'Don't you 'boy' me! You tricked me, you... you bastard!'

'Oh, cut it out. I'd say I'm sorry, but does Death not come for us all? And this one-,' he said, nodding to the Dark One, '-makes my job that little bit easier. Don't hate me. I'm not the bad guy here, I'm just an inevitability. Keep your mouth shut.'

The Dark One looked rattled.

'Stop filling the air with obfuscation! Through smoke and mirrors I must wade to see a scene so simple.'

Vincent and Mr Muerte stared at the Dark One, glanced at one another, then stared back at the Dark One.

'Ahem.' The Lord of Shadow cleared his throat. 'One just wasn't ready for a guest quite so soon, that's all. One needed time to make... preparations.'

He walked over to a nearby pillar. Mr Muerte stepped slyly to the side.

'There just seems to be some internal inconsistency, that's all,' Vincent added.

'See, this is why I don't like children,' said the Dark One. 'Always picking at things, always asking questions. Always asking *why*.

'Well, I'll tell you why. I need you here for as long as possible, understand? I need you here, withering away, until there's nothing left of you but a dried out husk and I'm strong enough to break through into your world, correct? Yes. So there I am thinking: the last thing I want is you turning up early. Not that I had anything to worry about, clearly. You're about as formidable as a damp sock.

'So I had you thrown off the train. It seemed as good a plan as any, leaving you to wander the desert. But *then* I thought: where better to keep you than close by? Anything could have happened out there. You could have been cooked under the sun, or squashed under the foot of a giant. Who knows what's going through that head of yours. And so I had Mr Muerte bring you here, but not a moment before I had everything prepared.'

Vincent thought about this for a moment. "Prepared" didn't seem so friendly a word when eight legs hung disembodied from the rafters.

'When you say "prepared"...?' he asked.

'Well you can't invite a guest to stay and not have a room ready for them, can you?'

The Dark One pressed a stone upon the pillar and it slid in with a satisfyingly small clink. The slab of rock beneath Vincent's feet swung open, revealing a chute stretching into darkness below.

For the slightest second he remained motionless in the air, like a marionette hung by strings.

And then he fell - down, down and down.

CHAPTER THIRTY

Grandma put her needles down in the middle of a garter stitch. Something was very wrong.

The scarf would have to wait.

Something had been amiss since the day that girl had died. It wasn't just that Vincent wasn't himself - that would have been expected of anyone. No, a darkness had sensed his vulnerability. Like she'd said, children are the most malleable. It's easy to apply pressure and watch the fissure spread between this world... and whatever lies beyond. That's when the nightmares had started.

A simple bit of psychology would have done the trick. It *did* do the trick, actually, until her daughter had been stupid enough to throw the blasted dreamcatcher into the bin. All in the boy's head or not, it wasn't wise to let that sort of darkness spread. An imagination could be far more real than people realised.

And now she had that worried feeling in her stomach. Just fantastic.

She put on some warmer layers and put everything she needed into her bag. A quick glance at the clock said it was almost ten. It was getting pretty late but the buses would still be running. *That's the good thing about being retired*, she thought. *Nobody ever tells you off for staying out all night.*

She picked up her house keys from the bowl by the front door, then paused. She went back into the living room and retrieved her knitting needles from the armchair, popping them into her bag alongside everything else. You never knew when you might need something sharp.

She locked her door and followed the road down to the bus stop. The next ride was only three minutes away. She huddled in the shelter, clutching her bag to her lap.

She got on the number 207, and sat in the seat closest to the front. Two young men in hoodies and baseball caps shared the row to the back, in fits of giggles over their own intoxication. Their fool's guffaws filled the bus as much as their abundant, sour aftershave. She huddled in her seat, clutching her bag even closer to her lap until the straps were little more than taut, leather worms.

A half hour journey saw her arrive at the hospital at almost a quarter to eleven. Stars were struggling to shine through the light pollution, blinking like the cars in the multi-storey. Grandma didn't find hospitals the most enticing of places to begin with, but there was something a little unnerving about them after dark. A little too clean, and a little too empty.

She walked past the book stores and fast food outlets and made her way to Vincent's ward. The nurse at the desk politely reminded her that visiting hours were between so and so, and she politely reminded the nurse that as a grandmother she would go where she damn well pleased. The nurse decided to turn a blind eye, as it seemed preferable to losing one.

She gasped as she walked into Vincent's room. Her heart fluttered like a moth burning in a candle flame.

Vincent was in his bed, exactly as she'd seen him last. But his hair was plastered against his forehead with sweat, and the room was many shades too dark. She flicked the light switch but the room only went from dark to not-so-dark, the fluorescent strips flickering a pale, dying light.

She ambled over to his bedside as quickly as possible, dragging the room's most comfy chair alongside her. Sitting down, she felt his brow, which burned against the back of her hand. Yep. Something was definitely wrong.

The nightmares were still finding their way into the boy.

She considered calling for the nurse, but stopped the first syllable from climbing out her mouth. Her gut told her that this was no ordinary fever. Dim lighting that felt ripped straight from a B-movie horror flick didn't put her at ease either. She quietly shut the door, dampened one of the towels from the adjoining bathroom and dabbed Vincent's forehead with it.

The darkness was syphoning everything from him. He was being shaped, torn apart, thrown like a tattered rag. Whether he was trying to come back or not, he was losing. It was bad enough that whatever horrors plagued the boy were spreading into reality, but she wasn't going to lose her little grandson.

She took her needles from out of her bag and began to knit.

CHAPTER THIRTY-ONE

Vincent found himself lying face-down on the floor so often that he started to wonder if it would be easier to just stay there. He could crawl from place to place, and cut out the falling entirely.

He let himself lie motionless for a few minutes. He felt he deserved it.

He was in what could well have been the most bland room of all time. It was so bland that it almost became interesting in how bland it was. Four walls, one ceiling, one floor. All stone. There were no windows and as such no light, but Vincent could see all the same. Everything was the epitome of grey.

He'd been thrown into the dungeons. Brilliant. Just brilliant.

He thought he'd let himself continue being horizontal for just a little bit longer.

There wasn't much point in moving, not really. He'd been so close, but when he needed to act and take control he'd just let everything play out like a scene in front of him. He was useless, pathetic, stupid. He'd lost. He'd failed. He had an eternity in a stone cell to look forward to. He could hardly wait.

He dragged his head along the floor just far enough to look up at the wall furthest away. There was an iron cell door in its centre, complete with sliding slot for peeping through. It looked very heavy, and very locked.

Maybe it was better just to stop. Stop chasing, stop trying to make sense of it all.

Just stop.

He shut his eyes.

He saw cities bathed in darkness. He saw countryside up in flames. He saw hideous creatures as big as streets, stork-like legs straddling buildings, crushing people underfoot. Lashing tentacles, needled teeth and bodies torn asunder. Nightmares held the world in a palm belonging to that King of Terrors, the Dark One. He sat upon his throne, his shark grin relishing the misery.

And you know what? Vincent didn't care. Everybody was going to die anyway, sooner or later. It was just a matter of time. And it wasn't as if he was going to suffer the same fate, given his current incarceration.

He wondered what would happen to him. Would he remain here forever, trapped in his own little pocket of time? Or would he fade away once the Dark One was through? He supposed the more tangible the creeper became, the less tangible he would become. Eventually he'd just be an echo.

Oh well. There are probably worse ways to go.

It was bad enough not knowing what time it was in this godforsaken world, or not knowing how quickly it was passing. But the outside didn't compare to the cell. Without the sun as his guide he could have been in there for hours without a clue; for all he knew he'd been there minutes.

Lying with his face to the stone wasn't actually very comfortable, so Vincent decided to pick himself up. Only as far as a sitting position, mind. He slumped with his back against one of the walls.

Well, this is it. Better get used to it.

Suddenly there was a noise like an iron door opening and slamming shut, yet his own remained stuck fast. The scrambling of hands and feet across the floor, then silence. And in that silence it was clear where the noise had come from: beyond the wall to his right.

Vincent got down on his hands and knees and approached the wall. It was, as already mentioned, a particularly uninspiring structure, without even the tally charts or madman's etchings one would expect from such a surface. It was cold, flat, monolithic stone.

But right down at its bottom, hiding down by the floor, was a tiny, rectangular grate.

He pressed his eye to the hole, wondering what he might see.

Another eye, it just so happened. And a tuft of hair, bound by pink ribbon.

'Oh, it's you again.'

'Hey, Vincent!' came Lily's peppy voice. 'Aren't you pleased to see me?'

'To be honest I'm tired, and I'd quite like to be left alone.'

'Oh come on, don't be like that. It's not all that bad.'

'I'm trapped in a stone cell in a dreamworld talking to a dead person. It is exactly that bad. How on earth are you so chipper?'

'Probably because I'm dead, I suppose. Things don't tend to matter all too much after that.'

Vincent sat up and stared into space.

'I can't bring you back home, can I?' he asked.

'No,' Lily replied, 'I don't think you can.'

'It's not fair.'

'No, it isn't.'

'I mean, it's not so bad for you. Like you said, you're dead. I'm the one left here, dealing with the fallout.'

'Oh, great. Make me feel bad, why don't you.'

Vincent curled his hands into fists. As much as he'd wanted her back, he didn't know what to say.

'Do you think it gets any easier?'

'Not easier, no. I guess you just adjust to it over time.'

'Yeah, I guess so. Probably how my mum felt about my dad, or my grandpa.'

'Yes, probably.'

'Do you ever think about what could have been? I mean, what could have happened in your future?'

'Not since dying, no. But you obviously do, otherwise I wouldn't be here and we wouldn't be having this conversation. So please, go ahead.'

'Alright, smarty pants. But just imagine, the two of us going through school, going to university, getting married-'

'Who said we were getting married?'

'Oh calm down, I meant to different people. But can't you imagine that? I can't get my head around the idea that none of those things will happen.'

'Well nobody can tell what the future *will* hold, Vincent, let alone what a future *could* have held. Who says we would have stayed friends? What's to say we would have gone to the same university? And - and this is a big and - who's to say I would want to get married to a stinky boy?'

'I'd like to think we would have stayed friends 'til the end.'

'And we did, Vincent. I think you'll find we did.'

Vincent sat in silence for a while. He felt more at peace than before, but still there seemed to be a part of him missing. Wounds take time to heal, he supposed.

'Why are you down here, anyway?' he asked.

No response.

'I said, why are you-'

'No need to shout,' came a much older, quieter voice. 'I'm old, not deaf.'

A spider crawled out from the grate, no greater than a soda can from leg to leg. It scuttled up upon the back of Vincent's hand, which he duly raised to his face.

'Perhaps you just thought I was really far away. I'm actually just small.'

'Mother Spider?'

'I am she, in the flesh.'

'But you're dead. I saw the Dark One tear all your legs off.'

'Oh yes, that was me. Definitely dead. That was not a pleasant experience, I'll tell you that for free.'

'Then how are you here?'

'Well I'm in your head, aren't I. It's not like I have anywhere else to go.'

'Then let's talk about where you've been. Did you see Lily through there?'

'Lily? Who's Lily? Oh, you mean that girl. You're not still whining about her, are you?'

'Hey! Did you see her or not?'

'No, I didn't. There's nobody there, just stonework.'

'Oh.'

'Come on, boy. Turn that frown upside down. It's not all bad.'

'Why does everyone keep saying that?'

'Because you can't sit around moping forever. You don't see me crying just because somebody ripped all my legs off.'

'I just can't get my head around it. Death, I mean. It's so... finite.'

'Yes, it is. It's the most certain, finite thing of all. But there's one way we all live on.'

'Yeah?' Vincent could feel the conversation taking a turn for the cheesy.

'In the memories of others.'

Yep, there it was. Gorgonzola Central.

'Oh save me the life lessons,' he replied.

'I'm trying to help you get home, you bloody idiot! There's very little we can leave behind. The very best we can hope for is to leave a little part of ourselves in our wake, through the hearts and memories of others.

'Tell me, Vincent. What scenes lie painted within your head?'

Vincent thought of the good times. He thought back to when they first met in class, hating on every sum in Mathematics. He thought back to their lunch breaks sitting on the school steps, sharing chocolate buttons and swapping tales of the television they'd watched the night before.

He remembered her birthday party, and everyone running around laughing. There were cakes and party rings and sausage rolls. Balloons hung on strings, their escape foiled. There had been a giant bouncy castle, even though Lily couldn't really go on it. Not properly. He had somersaulted and backflipped and generally thrown himself about. He'd smiled so hard that his face hurt for the rest of the day.

He thought of the good times, and those memories were warm.

'I...'

He looked down, but his hand was empty. Mother Spider had gone.

'Oh.'

'Sorry, you were about to say something?' came a voice as powerful as a supernova, as deep as a black hole.

Mr Muerte stood in the corner of the cell, twiddling with his scythe.

'What? Where did you come from?' said Vincent.

'I'm everywhere, boy, don't you realise?' Mr Muerte said in his spookiest voice. 'There's nowhere I cannot find you.'

Vincent responded with his stoniest expression.

'Fine, suit yourself. I make an effort to stay in character and nobody appreciates it.'

'You gave me up to the Dark One!'

'You gave *yourself* up, I think you'll find. You're the one who wanted to go there, I merely facilitated the process. At least I didn't request a finder's fee, then you really would be in trouble.'

'I seem to be in enough trouble as it is, thanks to you.'

'Are you? Are you actually? Because it seems to me that you're just sitting there, moping, preferring to believe yourself in trouble than actually put the effort into picking yourself up. Stop going around in circles, boy.'

Vincent got to his feet and walked right up to Mr Muerte's smiling face (or lack thereof). His cloak ebbed and flowed like the darkest fog but Vincent simply wasn't frightened anymore.

'I'm trapped in a box and I'm being used as a vessel for a Nightmare King to travel into the real world. Tell me why I shouldn't be moping, please.'

'Have you tried the door?'

'...what?'

'The door. The door right there. I assume you've noticed it?'

'...Yes. But it's locked, isn't it?'

'Well I wouldn't presume to know. Perhaps you should give it a try, instead of sitting in the corner talking to a spider about the past.'

Vincent went to reach for the door, but stopped himself. Something didn't seem right, or at least seemed less right than usual.

'Why are you helping me now?' he asked.

'I was helping you every step of the way, you strange child. You had to go through this. Nobody walks along this path and finds it easy. There's denial; there's anger. You'll beg and bargain and you'll lose. It's step by painful step. But eventually you'll climb out of the hole; it just takes a little while to find the hand grooves.'

Mr Muerte straightened himself up and adjusted his cloak.

'Like I said,' he continued, 'I'm not the bad guy. I'm just an inevitability.'

Vincent felt the cold metal beneath his fingertips. The door sure *felt* locked tight. He guessed there was only one way to find out.

'You know,' he said to Mr Muerte, 'you're not all that bad really.'

'Thanks, kid. I've always thought people got the wrong impression.'

The door opened.

CHAPTER THIRTY-TWO

Well it wasn't quite how she'd imagined it would turn out, but it would have to do.

Grandma held her creation out in front of her. Even with her decades of practice, she had never been all that great at speed-knitting. It had always seemed a little counter-intuitive, in that the more she practiced the older she got and the older she got the slower she became. She hadn't thought of knitting as something required in an emergency.

It was thin and fragile, but perhaps that was the point. A thick rim ran in a perfect circle, but loose straggling threads dangled precariously below. In its centre ran row upon row of criss-crossing yarn. It looked like the world's worst tennis racket.

It didn't share too much likeness to a dreamcatcher, but the essentials were there. It was probably unlikely that the hospital had any feathers lying around, so she'd had to make do with what she had to hand. A lot of red wool, it had turned out.

It would probably work. Maybe.

She felt Vincent's forehead. It was still hot, hotter perhaps than before. Beads of sweat rolled down his forehead and pooled upon the pillow.

She draped the dreamcatcher across his duvet so that it covered his chest; she straightened out the rogue threads so that they reached out towards his feet. The lights were still blinking on and off, and even when on their light was only so strong as to cast a silver glow over the outlines of the room.

Grandma had closed the blinds across the windows. If anybody had walked down the corridor they would have seen a witch performing a satanic ritual on some poor coma patient. It would have been very hard to explain. Luckily it was the middle of the night and the hospital was as quiet as a silent disco in a library. Only the occasional squeak of a porter's trolley broke the emptiness, and the nurse had long ago stopped paying any sort of attention.

More dabbing of the forehead with a damp towel.

She took Vincent's hand in her own and gave it a squeeze. They say a coma patient can still experience the world outside, they just can't react to it. Perhaps Vincent heard her knitting away, her needles click clacking together like a tap dancer. Perhaps that would have calmed him, made him feel at home. Perhaps he could smell her perfume, which he'd always thought was a magnitude of ten too strong. And perhaps he could feel her hand around his, and know that she was there with him. Know that she would guide him back home the best she could.

Or perhaps there was nothing going on inside anymore, and she was holding on to nothing but flesh and bone. But her little grandson had to be in there somewhere, he had to be.

She sat back in her chair and fished out a half-eaten packet of toffees from her bag. It was going to be a long night.

CHAPTER THIRTY-THREE

For what should have been a stoney, underground corridor, there sure was a lot of breeze. And snow, for that matter.

Vincent looked back into the cell. Yep, there were still the same four walls, though no sign of Mr Muerte. He looked around at his new surroundings, and had to blink off a snowflake that sat upon his eyelashes. He shivered as if ice cubes had been dropped down the back of his shirt.

Yep, he wasn't in the tower anymore.

The inside was a cell but the outside was a Victorian carriage, complete with curtained windows and wooden fittings. On each side to the front and back swayed a single lantern, stroking an orange glow upon the passing landscape. The wheels bucked and rocked their way over the stony trail. Vincent had to hold on to the door to avoid falling off.

To every side was a near-vertical cliff, reaching up beyond the clouds. Boulders and icy stalagmites served as the mountains' picket fence, and though their peaks were amongst the stars their toupees of snow extended almost down to the road. Those snowflakes that fell dissipated upon touching the floor like cotton candy in the rain.

There was little light now, and storm clouds seemed to blanket the sky. Only a glimmer of sun sparkled on the horizon; all else was inky and gloom. Outside the gaze of the lanterns, everything had started to resemble etchings in black canvas. And when the storm clouds crackled electric blue, shapes could be seen stalking through the darkness.

First Vincent made out a leg, a league in height and as thin as a crane's. He heard its footstep crash through the snow like muffled thunder. A tail, snaking between the mountains, as long as a summer's stream. And then a flash of disembodied teeth, a momentary megalodon smile hanging in the heavens.

At first there was only one. Then amongst the forks of lightning came another, and another, and another, until the skies were filled with colossus upon colossus. Some were tall and thin, others small and vicious - all wandered the peaks hungry.

As the darkness grew, the beasts came out to play.

The carriage rolled ever onwards, meandering down the winding path. A moment later it passed a rickety old sign, savaged by time and embedded in the rocks, waving in the wind like a dog shaking off snow. It read:

The Big Ridge: Abandon Lyfe Ye Who Goes Yonder

Vincent needed a better view point. He climbed up the door using the locks as footholds, and clambered up onto the carriage's roof. It was tricky not to fall; each stone that went under the wheels caused the whole vehicle to heave and buck like a cantankerous donkey. He slipped once, grazing his shin against the rusty iron frame.

With arms and legs spread as far apart as possible without slipping and doing the splits, he drew himself to as full a height as he could manage.

Oh God-bloody-dammit.

He could make out the tower, so that was a relief. It just happened to be the most infinitesimally small unit of relief imaginable, washed down with a considerable mixer of despair. The tower was so far away, so small in the distance, that it barely measured more than an eyelash's breadth on the horizon. If it hadn't stretched high into the clouds above he probably wouldn't have noticed it, so hidden it was amongst the storm.

So much for keeping him close by. Just another trick from the Dark One, Vincent supposed.

Or perhaps he feels too threatened to have me close.

It made sense. No other reason to send him away when he already had him trapped. He must have hoped that Vincent would stay in the cell for eternity, wasting away as far from salvation as possible.

Well that wasn't going to happen, *no sir*.

Though how he was going to go about making it un-happen was a whole other kettle of fish. The carriage was travelling in the opposite direction at quite some pace. And it wasn't as if walking was much of an option, even if he managed to avoid breaking his neck jumping from the roof. It wasn't as if he could just ask the carriage to stop.

Wasn't it?

He made his way back to the front of the carriage, arms spread wide like the least aerodynamic plane, and looked down at the driving seat.

He rather wished he hadn't.

There, gripping the reins as if through rigor mortis, was one of the oxen men from the Rooma Express' furnace. Still he wore no shirt, his chest bare to the tundra. His back was frozen to the leather seat, fastened in by icicles. This time his skin wasn't bronze but the lightest, palest blue. With his bald head and hulking form he looked like some weird, alien giant.

At the end of his reins was a single ram the size of a horse, curly horns and all. Vincent didn't know why he expected anything else.

'Er, excuse me?' he asked.

The man turned slowly, as if made of plaster and liable to crumble at any moment. The ram kept pace and followed the path, even when the driver took his eyes from off it.

Well, eyes may have been a generous noun.

His counterparts in the train furnace had ones that were glassy and hollow, but this man had eyes that were truly empty. It wasn't as if he didn't have them, but that he had the *opposite* of eyes - unseeing voids that looked without thought. He stared straight through Vincent, never blinking, as if he were nothing of consequence. As if he weren't there at all. And then he turned back, as gradually as he had turned before.

Vincent supposed he wasn't the stopping sort.

So much for diplomacy then. Vincent bunched his hands into fists. Why did the world have a habit of being the most frustrating just when he had the least patience? He looked around for something blunt and sturdy.

Unfortunately he found nothing of the sort.

Fortunately, he found something considerably more painful.

The lanterns were swinging wildly now, threatening to fly off their hooks. Vincent did one of them a favour, and eased it free of its confinement. Its fiery glow cast a bonfire aura around him, and for a split second Vincent felt quite content to just bask in its warmth. Then he remembered what he was doing, bobbed its iron weight in his hand, and swung it around with all his might.

And boy, was it satisfying.

It connected with the man's head with a catastrophic crash, though his head must have been made of stronger stuff than the lantern as it was the latter that shattered. Vincent felt the handle fly from his grasp and off into the passing snow bank, and shielded his eyes with his free arm as glass stabbed towards each point of the compass. Embers fell like golden rain.

The man simply banked left with the impact and, rather than turn around in an understandably furious rage, dropped to the stony trail below like a cannonball off a kitchen table. It didn't seem to have much effect on the carriage though, which maintained its breakneck descent through the winding valley path.

Nursing a bruised and slightly burned hand, Vincent dropped down to where the strange man had been sitting. He sat down upon the frosted leather and grabbed the flailing reins as they whipped back and forth, just in time to look up at the road ahead.

Or distinct lack of it.

Where there should have been road, there was not. No walkway, no path, not even a dirt trail in the rough. What *was* there, was a huge, massive, overwhelming lack of anything at all. A chasm, jagged and leagues deep. And yet the ram ahead of the reins kept charging on, ever faster.

Vincent was suddenly very aware that he hadn't the slightest clue how to ride a horse or drive a carriage or in fact do anything involving an animal and/ or wheels.

Forty metres from the cliff edge, approaching fast.

He wrenched the reins back as tight and viciously as he could. That seemed the right thing to do.

Twenty metres.

At first it seemed that the ram would charge on forever, but suddenly it reared up on its hind legs and dug them into the gravel. The momentum of the carriage sent its hooves ploughing through the dirt like a farmer's fork, its front legs treading the air above.

Ten metres.

And then a stop.

The rear wheels of the carriage rose into the air, then walloped back into the earth. The ram dropped back to its usual four legs. Vincent, however, flew through the air and landed just shy of the vertical drop by about five feet, skidding to a muffled rest in the depths of a nearby snow bank.

He scrambled to his feet, emerging from the snow accompanied by an expression akin to that of a caveman waking up in New York City, and put some distance between himself and the cliff face. He felt wobbly just looking at the serrated rocks below, whole mountain peaks of their own.

The ram munched on a dead weed.

Vincent looked at the carriage. One of the wheels had splintered pretty badly in the stop, and another looked as if it wouldn't last more than another mile or two before rolling off on its own accord.

That ram looks pretty intact though.

It looked up at Vincent with a face full of suspicion and a mouth full of browned dandelion, then returned to its meal.

Vincent pottered over and examined the mechanisms holding the ram and the carriage in place. It seemed to comprise mostly of leather buckles, which he prised quite easily from around the beast's belly. The straps fell to the floor, much to the ram's continued ignorance. It flicked its ear as snowflakes began to settle.

Vincent made his approach slowly, and lifted one leg in readiness to leap upon its back.

'Are you going to ask before you jump on? Most would at least buy me a drink first.'

Vincent removed his hands from the ram's knotted wool and turned to look at its questioning, horned face.

'Does everything with a mouth around here know how to talk?' said Vincent.

'Perhaps you'd find out if you cared to ask.'

There was a particularly awkward silence broken only by the steady rumbling of the ram's digestive system. The dandelion was no more.

'Look, I'm really short on time,' said Vincent, exhausted by all the anthropomorphic symbolism. 'I need to get back to the tower and save the day or something. I know it's not your fault that the carriage took me all the way out here, but could you please give me a lift back? *Please?'*

The ram cocked its head in thought.

'Yeah sure, why not. The food round here's terrible.'

The ram lowered its back and allowed Vincent to climb on top. Its wool was so fluffy and comfortable, like sitting in a blanket of candy floss and feathers, stitched together with kindness. He didn't know if it was the proper thing to do, but he held the ram's horns in each hand like bicycle handles.

'Now, down to business. Given that you're on a mission to save the world, or whatever,' said the ram, 'I'll only charge you the mate's rate. Call it a Hero Discount, or whatever. So that should be...'

'How about I don't lamp you?'

'Or that would work. Beggars can't be choosers, I suppose.'

The ram reared up on its hind legs and Vincent held on tight, almost slipping down its back and onto the dirt. Then it twisted on the spot and darted in the direction from which the carriage had come, no longer held back by its slow, spatially-inconsistent weight.

They were off.

Vincent kept his head down as much as possible, feeling the wind tear at him with the force of a jet engine. Both his face and clothes responded in much the same rippling fashion. His eyes felt as if the rest of his head would be torn free from them. The path ahead zipped from side to side as they barrelled along it, and the mountains passed by in a grey-white blur.

It didn't take long to pass the driver at the side of the road. He was sitting up amongst the snow and rocks, his face as deadpan as ever. There was something sad and pathetic in his aloneness though, and a considerable lump was forming on the back of his head. Vincent almost felt a little bad. Not enough to stop, of course.

They passed the wooden sign, which felt obliged to spin in the traditional, comic fashion.

And soon enough the mountains grew smaller and smaller and fewer and fewer, until their valleys became snowy hills and boulders became rocks. The howling of the wind grew quieter, and the falling snow came to a gradual stop. Patches of dry, dead grass poked through the white carpet, then banished it altogether.

Vincent could see the tower more clearly now that the peaks of the mountains had retreated. It stood as a knotted, knobbly bar joining the earth and the sky, holding up the heavens' weight. But it was also just one more black tower in a sea of many. The legs of the giant beasts that roamed beyond the Big Ridge were in the desert also, making a slow, thundering approach of their own.

It seemed that the Dark One wouldn't be crossing through alone.

The ram didn't slow for a moment. It charged between the Nightmare beasts' various appendages and broke out from the bush into sand and stone. No longer did the yellow sand burn underfoot but freeze in midnight silver, cloaked by the clouded canopy. A dust cloud rose in their wake, a bullet trail amongst the morbid calm of the arid wasteland.

CHAPTER THIRTY-FOUR

Lightning crackled and tore its way through the sky, stabbing indiscriminately at tower and bird of prey alike. A sudden squawk and burst of feathers signified another successful shot on target.

The Dark One stood at the top of his castle, at the pinnacle of his elegant tower of terror, arms stretched wide like a maniacal Doctor Frankenstein as fork upon fork of deadly charge licked the stonework around him. His grin - as deadly as a shark's, as insane as a Cheshire cat's - practically stretched in a full circle around his head. He couldn't have been happier.

The boy was gone. Not *gone* gone of course, no; he didn't want him dead. A lifeless corpse was no good at all. A mangled, mutilated, just-about-hanging-on-to-life almost-corpse that was a hundred miles away, now *that* was spot on. With any luck the carriage would have already plummeted into the depths beyond the Big Ridge, and with that the boy would be no trouble at all.

Another streak of lightning lashed down at his feet and the Dark One considered a hearty, villainous laugh, but ultimately thought it a little too much.

There were some massive creatures down below. Really, truly massive - as big as a diplodocus at least. It was impressive. The darker the clouds had gotten, the bigger the monsters had become... and the quicker they'd come plodding from out behind the mountains. With some of these goliaths following him into the human world, he'd barely need those scurrying fools in their hooded gowns. Well, they were good for a bit of grovelling, he supposed.

The static had left the air tasting sharp and purple. He liked it.

But what King is King without a Kingdom? What King indeed.

He looked straight up. It was so close.

Deep in the clouds there lay a fissure, bursting with shadowy, oily black. It writhed and thrusted like shapes on the brink of imagination, like silhouettes intertwined in ecstasy and agony, like larvae from dimensions only dreamt of. It was opening and closing, stretching, tearing itself between the two worlds. Between the world of Rooma, and everything else.

He'd seen a glimpse of the other side, and now he had the hunger.

So much misery to be sown, so much misery to reap.

God, it was almost too much. The Dark One had to restrain himself from jumping up and down. It just wouldn't do if one of the minions came up and saw him.

Soon. All it took was a tiny spoonful of that most elusive of ingredients: patience. He stretched an arm out and could almost touch the void's emptiness, it was so near. Soon.

Soon.

CHAPTER THIRTY-FIVE

With a screeching halt the ram arrived at the tower, and Vincent had to hold on tight to avoid being thrown from his ride a second time. The lumbering behemoths were still a fair way behind them; the ram had set a record pace.

The ram was also slumped against the floor and struggling for breath, however.

Vincent jumped from off its back just as the ram dropped to its side, its tongue lolling out from its mouth. Vincent felt truly awful.

'Oh, Mr. Ram, I'm so sorry,' he said. 'You shouldn't have pushed yourself so hard - I didn't know…'

'Don't worry about it,' wheezed the ram, its chest rising and falling feebly. 'It happens to me all the time.'

And with that, the ram died.

And then it jumped back up again.

'See? Good as new,' it said, bouncing up and down like a toddler on sugar.

Vincent stood with a mouth like the hole in a doughnut.

'Oh don't be so hard on yourself, kid,' the ram added, trotting around. 'It's part of the daily routine.'

It nodded once, and solemnly.

'Good luck saving everything. I'll be off now, if it's all the same to you.'

And then it was - off, that is. Sprinting through the desert like a cat splashed with water, looking for the next dandelion to satisfy its protesting digestive system.

Strange creature, thought Vincent. *But I suppose it would be stranger if it weren't.*

He looked up, and sure enough the three vultures circled about a dozen or so metres overhead. Their choreographed swooping did little to inspire confidence. His declining confidence certainly inspired hunger in the vultures.

What had his mother always said about bullies? Ah yes. Ignore them and they tend to go away. Or was that scabs?

With the ram but a speck in the distance, Vincent turned to the tower. It was taller than ever, darker than ever, more insurmountably stoney than ever. The rocks and squares that made up its walls were building more slowly now, so its construction must have been drawing to a close. There was a strong sensation of deja vu, but yet something had changed.

The statues that flanked the top of the steps had been completed, the whirlwind of pebbles and grit having long finished its sculpturing. The figures didn't strike a heroic pose, nor did they depict the Dark One towering over his victims. They simply showed Lily, her hair in bunches, her head bowed and shy. Enshrined in stone and utterly, eternally lifeless.

He hurried past them and pushed open the doors to the great hall, which voiced their creaky excitement at appearing in the story once more.

Now *this* was how a great hall should be. Very quiet, very empty, and very, very suspicious.

His footsteps echoed off the walls like a ping-pong ball shot into a tupperware box. Gone were the hooded figures and their bumbling; gone were the wooden scaffoldings. The entrance hall was complete, and yet abandoned.

Vincent made his way over to the left of the room, and peered into the hole through which he had fallen. It was long, and dark. He felt an overwhelming urge to jump down, though for the life of him couldn't say why. He tore his gaze away for fear of toppling in.

He went over to where Mother Spider's body had been, where her legs had hung like bloody piñata worms. He had to admit that they'd done a great job with the clean-up; not a single drop of blood stained the stone floor or ran amongst the cracks. Who knows what they'd done with the body. Was there a body? Oh, it confused Vincent's head just thinking about it.

The pillars shook and pebbles fell from the ceiling like hailstones.

He needed to get upstairs, quickly. He suspected there wasn't an express elevator anywhere, but there was a castle stairwell adorned with flaming torches. The first set of two pointed downwards, which seemed odd. But the others stood straight up. The golden glow amongst the gloom, it seemed almost… hopeful.

Vincent tried looking up but the helix stairs gave no hint as to the height of the tower. He stretched his legs and then started the climb.

* * *

What was it with architects and making steps that are too high for human legs? Who was this castle built for, a giraffe?

Vincent's legs burned with exhaustion. He looked back down the way he'd come, but that didn't fill him with any extra energy. He could only see five steps up and five steps down; he couldn't say if he'd climbed a mile or still had a mile to climb. Either way, he didn't know if his legs could manage much more. His muscles had turned to wood. Perhaps he should have been born a pelican.

He sat on the nearest step to take a breath. Even a journey up a dumbwaiter shaft would have been preferable to this.

The shadows upon the wall three feet below flickered against the glow of the fires. Then another flicker. Then a whole wave of flickering until shapes could be made out like puppets behind a screen - strange, angry puppets.

The Dark One's hooded minions were charging up the stairs behind him.

'Oh, give me a break,' muttered Vincent, climbing to his feet.

He could hear them shouting, though much of that may have been involuntary as a result of climbing over one another and falling back down the stairs, rather than through any real aggression. Vincent decided he didn't want to find out.

Suddenly he seemed reinvigorated. He bounded up the stairs like a gazelle from a lion, albeit a gazelle that had to keep spinning round and round and round on the poles of the tiniest carousel. He felt a bit sick, but he put a pin in it. There didn't seem to ever be the time.

He looked over his shoulder. The shadows were larger, and formed from unpleasant shapes.

He felt his foot slipping as soon as he put it down. The stonework was weak, and the step only a couple of centimetres wide on the inside. One second the toe of his shoe was balanced on its precipice, the next it was his knee smashing into it. He felt the skin tear and the warm trickle of blood run down his shin. He picked himself up. He had the same feeling he got whenever he had to go upstairs after turning the light out; that a hand would reach out, grab his ankle and drag him back down.

The walls flashed by in a blur, and with a sudden slam Vincent found himself at the end of the stairwell. He peeled his face from off the solid oak door and pushed it open.

Or rather, he went to push it open. The door wouldn't budge.

His hands scrambled around looking for a latch, a lock, a wooden bar in a deadlock, *anything* that could explain why the door remained as stubborn as his Mother past nine o'clock. But there was nothing, not even a keyhole. It seemed to remain shut simply because it didn't want to open.

The screams of the minions came roaring up the stairwell. Despite themselves they were making quick progress, and the shadows loomed longer than ever. Vincent could swear he heard giggling and crying amongst the rage, but that hardly made it any less frightening.

He rattled the door some more, but it metaphorically put its foot down. Vincent responded by giving it a hefty kick. It seemed to give a little.

Louder voices from below, getting closer. It seemed some were scraping weapons along the walls. At least, he hoped it was weapons they were scraping.

He ran at the door with his shoulder. It creaked but still it stayed in place. A second attempt at ramming yielded similar results. He rubbed his shoulder, which already felt unappreciated enough to offer a bruise in return. His heart felt like machine gun fire.

He backed up down the stairwell and, feeling various eyes bore into his back, charged head first into the door.

CHAPTER THIRTY-SIX

The door swung open with a splintering crack and Vincent stumbled through, surprised. He patted the floor with his hands as he struggled to remain upright, then darted back the way he'd lurched to slam the door back shut. A wooden beam lay cast aside nearby, so he quickly snatched it up and slotted it through the deadbolt. He rested with his back against the door, eyes shut and catching his breath. At just that moment there was an almighty boom as the collective minions slammed into the other side, hammering at it with their torches and elbows.

It shook and bulged, but it held.

A camera flash caught his eye, and the roar of a lion caught his ears. He suddenly remembered where he was.

Everything was so dark that even the shadows had shadows, and the blackness had taken on hues all of its own. There were light blacks and dark blacks; blacks that seemed deadly purple and other blacks that positively shined. The whole world seemed coated in treacle, though the world had grown very small indeed.

He stood atop the tower's battlements, a circular arena of stone and crenels. The wind was terrible up there, and the air as thin as tissue paper. The whole tower creaked and swayed like bulrushes in a river and everything smelled faintly of burning. Oh, and the whole place was suffocated by a vicious cycle of a storm cloud. From the sound of it, he was in the epicentre.

There was a single gargoyle to one side. For all its wings and fangs and the expression of a wet Monday morning, it didn't look half as unpleasant as the group still trying to push their way through the door behind.

A bolt of lightning came screeching down at the floor beside him, and Vincent leapt to the side like a cat with spring-legs. The stone was charred and smokey.

'Why, oh why, will you not just stay where you're put?'

The Dark One stood at the far side of the tower, his arms outstretched in disbelief. He struck a gaunt silhouette, tilting his head in jerky stop-motion as if lit up, frame by frame. His head was transfixed upon the vortex above, but his rake-like hands dropped to his sides.

'Oh well, it matters not,' he said, each word infused with wistful flight. 'It's too late to stop it now, much too late.'

'Look,' said Vincent in the most commanding voice a ten year old can muster, whilst walking towards the Dark One. 'This doesn't have to happen. There's plenty of room for you in here, and me out there.'

The Dark One laughed, and for the first time broke his gaze from the clouds.

'Oh child. You are foolish. Without you here, there is no here. The moment you step out from this world and into the next, all this is gone. Else there's only a glimpse I see, each time you shut those eyes of yours. So no, this does have to happen. It does, it is, and it will.'

Vincent thought he saw a twitch in the Dark One's side. A glitch, or some sort of struggle.

'But you don't belong there! That's my home, I don't want it to be as bad as here.'

'Well at least you won't have to get used to it. You'll be in that hospital bed until they pull the plug. Or I do, come to think of it.'

Another twist and bulge came and went in the body of the Dark One. Now that Vincent thought about it, he definitely seemed more tangible than before. More whole, he might say.

'No. I don't want this to bleed into the real world. I want this to stop *right now.*'

'Don't come crying to me about it. This is all your doing, after all. You're the only one that's keeping you here.'

Vincent stopped just as he was about to reply. The Dark One was right, though by the distractedly glazed look upon what constituted a face he hadn't yet realised what he'd said. Vincent *was* the only person keeping him here.

He was tired of this. He wanted to get back to his old life, his normal life, whether things had changed forever or not.

He tried shutting his eyes and relaxing, letting everything fade away from around him. He was bound to find himself awake in his bed, everything back as it should be.

It didn't work, obviously.

When he opened his eyes the Dark One was still standing there, only now his long, willowing fingers traced the very base of the clouds, sending sparks cascading as if from an axel grinder. The void was bigger and more open than ever, gaping above the terrible king like a hungry maw.

The banging at the staircase door was getting louder and louder. He didn't have much time.

Then Vincent noticed the strange movement within the Dark One for a third time, only on this occasion it wasn't so fleeting. Something was stretching out from his skin as if it were elastic - one tube, then another, then another. And suddenly Vincent realised that they weren't just simple shapes, but a hand. A small hand, reaching for help.

The fissure began to swallow the Dark One, descending inch by inch. Tentacles of oily black slapped and writhed around him.

Everything would have normally told Vincent not to plunge his hands into the amorphous body of a nightmare overlord, but as everything seemed to be wrong he had the unbreakable suspicion that it was right.

He ran towards the Dark One, dodging the slabs of ink that pounded into the stonework each way and everywhere. His target seemed too preoccupied to notice anymore, his jagged grin so wide it threatened to leave his face and branch out on a villainous campaign all of its own.

He grabbed the hand shaped lump and grimaced at the slimy oil that began to leak over his arm. The hand grabbed back and Vincent felt himself get pulled inside. The Dark One, at least, seemed not to notice. Vincent anchored himself to the floor and heaved, and at last felt some give.

He knew who would be coming out, of course. It could only be one.

Lily grew out of the Dark One's side like the cutest conjoined twin, though it was pretty grotesque all the same. She peeled away from the goo until her entire upper half hung loose, held in place only by Vincent's arms.

He expected her to be screaming, crying, panicking. But when she lifted her head all she had to show were smiles.

'Let me go, Vincent. It's okay. You have to let me go.'

Vincent froze. All he could offer in return were monosyllabic noises.

'You can't save me,' she continued. 'It's over, but that's okay. *You have to let me go.*'

His fingers didn't want to, but he knew he had to do it. It wasn't that he didn't have fight left in him, it's was just there was no battle left to fight. It was over and yes, it was okay.

Finally the door to the stairwell burst open, flying off its hinges and sending splinters in every direction like blow darts. The hooded figures spilled out with many a knee and elbow flailing, rushing at Vincent like flaming torch-wielding villagers after a monster.

The Dark One turned to face him suddenly, mouth torn into a roar, ready to tear and rip and shred.

Vincent let go.

There was a burst of blinding light, a pulse of pure white that rinsed through every stone and every wave in the air. It rocketed up from the Dark One's chest, a pillar of brilliance that pierced the void like a pike through flesh. The terrible king writhed and clawed, impaled to the spot, screaming and howling until he and the disturbed wind sang as one. The minions disappeared into the cyclone, swept away by the radiant tide.

It was so bright it burned. It felt like a brand against Vincent's skin, blistering and peeling. But it was good, somehow. It felt like a release, at last.

The oily tendrils bit down against the light, and then all there was was white.

CHAPTER THIRTY-SEVEN

It was half past three in the morning, and Grandma had utterly failed to stay awake. Long gone were the nights when she could stay up all hours partying. These days she was lucky to get through an episode of Downton Abbey without passing out.

She dreamt of times past and soap operas. She had no time for nightmares; the old have tackled all they need fear.

It was raining outside the window. Beads ran down the glass in slender brushstrokes. Night bled in and pooled across the floor.

Grandma awoke with a start. There were toffees scattered across her lap and the cold hospital floor. She tutted to herself and bent down to gather them up. Luckily they were individually wrapped, otherwise that would have been a terrible waste.

The wrappers lay like dull stones in the dark. Then, like stars blooming in the midnight sky, they began to sparkle. First blinking, then with a steady whine like the first breath of a generator, the fluorescent lighting waxed into life. Shadows retreated into the corners and back under the bed, and the silence was that little bit less empty.

'Grandma?' asked a small, tired voice.

She looked up and there he was, her little grandson, as well as he'd ever been. His little blue eyes, opening up again. His little hands, creaking open and closed, pinching the bridge of his nose as he rubbed his eyes awake.

'Oh, Vincent,' she said, rushing over to hug him. Between her crushing embrace and pungent perfume he came close to passing out again. He pushed himself free and scanned the room with bulging eyes.

'Where is he? Where is he?' he shouted, trying to push himself out of bed. He seemed stuck fast in a net, held back like a marionette. He looked down at his arms and saw tubes sticking out from them, snaking their way to the machines around him.

'It's okay, Vincent,' said Grandma, putting a reassuring hand on his shoulder. 'You're in the hospital, you're going to be okay.'

Vincent's breathing dropped from jackhammer level to that of somebody blowing up an air bed. His eyes stopped pinballing around the room and came to a gentle stop towards an old, familiar, wrinkled face.

'So he… he didn't make it through?' he asked.

'I don't know who *he* is, darling, but no.' She stroked the hair from off his forehead. 'There's only us two here.'

Vincent thrust his arms around his grandmother and sobbed. He didn't really know if he was happy or sad, he only knew he was relieved.

'Oh, Grandma,' rose muffled words from her chest, 'it was horrible. I was stuck in this nightmarish place and he wouldn't let me leave, and she was there and I just *couldn't get home…*'

Grandma looked at the crumpled bedsheets and saw the makeshift dreamcatcher sticking out of the folds.

No, she thought, *it couldn't be. It was just in his head - a terrible, terrible nightmare.*

But just perhaps?

'Don't worry, Vincent, you're safe now. Just try to relax, I'll get the doctor.'

'Don't leave me!'

'I won't, I promise,' she said, getting up slowly. 'I won't go any further than the door.'

She pulled it open and peered out towards the reception area. It was deserted, save for a cleaner pushing a trolley towards the elevators.

'Excuse me,' she called out. 'Excuse me? Can you fetch me a doctor, please? My grandson has just woken up.'

'Grandma? The Dark One said that he would come into the real world and turn everything into ruin, and Lily was there but I couldn't save her and...'

'Vincent,' said Grandma, returning to the bed. 'It was just a nightmare. No matter how real it seemed, no matter how horrible it may have felt, can I ask you to put it out of your mind? Your mother doesn't need to hear all that. She's been worried silly as it is. Can you do that for me?'

Vincent thought for a second, then nodded. *Yes. It wasn't real. A dream is a dream and nothing more, and what's in your head can't hurt you.*

'Sure, Grandma. Can I see her? Can I see my mum?'

'Sure, sweetness. Sure.'

Grandma returned to the door and spotted the cleaner returning to his trolley with a hurried doctor in tow.

'And I don't suppose I can trouble you for a phone, can I? I need to make a call.'

CHAPTER THIRTY-EIGHT

It didn't take long for Vincent to find himself waist high in sweets, chocolates and comic books. His mother found herself buying him everything in sight, and then struggling to justify a sugar embargo.

She'd received a phone call from Grandma at half three that morning. At first she'd almost thrown up with fear; the ringing phone at night brings only the worst news. With a shaking hand and a toiling stomach she'd risen the receiver to her ear, then screamed when she heard her boy was awake.

She'd gotten to the hospital just before sunrise. Chris had offered to drive them but she'd swept him out of the house in her rush to leave; it would have been too much of a shock for the poor boy. They would meet, but not at dawn in a hospital room.

That sick feeling hadn't really subsided, and her lungs felt like deflated balloons. But it was a good sickness, the sort that throws out all of the bad. And all that dissipated the moment she'd seen her little boy, sitting up and sucking on one of his grandmother's toffees. Seen his radiant smile as he saw her enter his room. Felt his arms and breath wrap around her neck.

Both she and Grandma had stayed whilst the doctors did their tests, though Grandma spent most of that time in a heavy nap. Nobody could offer any better explanation for Vincent's sudden recovery than they could for his coma in the first place, but they all agreed that his vitals were great across the board. He was going home.

And so here he was, back at the house as if nothing had ever happened. Perhaps it was just the attention and the sugar-high but Anna could swear that he was better than before the accident. His appetite had certainly returned with him, that much was obvious; when he wasn't hoovering up sherbet he was diving into his grandmother's spaghetti and meatballs. It finally seemed as if the world had drawn the curtains and let some sunshine into their lives.

It wouldn't ever go back to normal, not quite at least. Vincent still had his moments, the odd occasion when reality would kick in and memory would mimic the present. But it wasn't like before. He wasn't trapped inside himself anymore. He put on a smile and carried on. Everybody has to carry on.

And right now he was bouncing off the walls from too many strawberry laces.

* * *

The bell rang out across the field. Summers may seem as if they last forever, but summer lunch breaks certainly don't.

Vincent kicked the ball back to Simon and plunged his hand into the make-shift goalpost to fish out his jumper. He tied it around his waist, joined the queue to re-enter the classroom, and was promptly told to wear it like a normal person.

Lily's desk was still empty, as Mrs Henderson hadn't wanted to make anyone else feel weird by filling her spot. To Vincent, though, it felt more a memorial than it did an empty space. His lessons would always be missing something, but in time the hole would be less glaring. The number of secret messages exchanged had certainly taken a hammering, however.

'Vincent?'

'Mmm?' he replied, looking up.

'I asked you why we have seasons.' Mrs Henderson sounded exasperated. She was tapping her desk with her pen as well, which meant he'd better have been listening. Vincent didn't know what Mrs Henderson did in her lunch breaks but it sure left her in a foul mood afterwards.

'…Because the earth is tilted on its axis, making each hemisphere closer and further away at different times of the year?'

Mrs Henderson studied Vincent with her eyebrows for a moment. Then she conceded.

'Exactly right. Now, can anybody tell me…'

Vincent gazed back across the room. But he didn't just gaze at Lily's desk, no. He gazed out into the playing field, and wondered how long it would be until he was free to play outside once more.

* * *

It was weird meeting Chris, his mother's new… friend. But it wasn't a bad weird.

He seemed nice enough and Mum seemed happy. She certainly got scatty when he first came over to say hi. He'd never seen her so flustered. Vincent wasn't sold yet, but he'd give it time. He probably owed his mother that much at least.

And it would be nice for someone else to take care of her, for a change. He'd taken Grandma's advice and not mentioned what he'd seen in his dreams; he didn't want to concern her. It was all in the past and all in his head, after all.

Vincent's birthday party had been cancelled but Chris had taken them to the zoo instead, which immediately earned him brownie points. Vincent loved the zoo. Or rather, Vincent loved the animals. Nowhere else could you see so many exciting exotic beasts so close up... except perhaps out in the wild, he conceded. The tigers didn't *look* sad in their cages, though.

Neither did the pelicans or the rhinos or the hyenas or the meerkats or the rabbits. The vultures though, they did look sad. They always looked sad. Three huddled together on their branch, their bald heads shimmering under the summer sun. Vincent could have sworn they were grumbling under their breath.

* * *

A tiny ball of rock continued its long journey around its sun, peering distantly at each of its neighbours as they followed their own paths. And on that tiny galactic speck stood a great many hairless apes, thinking how lucky they were to be stood on that orb of grit, thinking such lucky thoughts.

All of them doing their damnedest to ignore a glaring, simple truth: that there really was no point in them or that rock at all. They created stories, they created hope and they made everything seem oh so important, but it made no real difference in the end. Nothing really matters, and everything ends.

And that's okay. We create stories and mythos and form friendships and partnerships because that's all we have, and that's all anybody *could* have. We might be hairless apes attributing meaning where there isn't any, mourning chance collections of atoms that collect for so small a time that, to the universe at large, they may as well not have existed at all. But that's all we have. Without connection, we succumb to that very nothingness. Without it we may as well not be.

One day that tiny ball of rock will stop following that journey, and by then all that we hold as important will be gone. Gone, and forgotten. None of it will matter; none of it will have ever mattered, not really. But until then we have to make the best of the fleeting time we have.

Legacy is all we can leave behind. The way we impact one another's lives as we sparkle and then fade out. The echoes heard by anybody left to hear.

Everyone's writing a story; everyone's filling up the pages of their book. Some will end as epics, others as short as a sonnet. But it cannot be said that a short story is any less beautiful. The beauty is all in the writing.

DENOUEMENT

It was half past nine at night, and all teeth were brushed and faces washed. Pyjamas were pulled on and bedcovers pulled right up under the chin.

Vincent felt like a pig wrapped in blankets, like a sausage in a bun. And it felt *good*. His mother tucked each edge of his duvet into the mattress until he was but a pea under paper, and fluffed his pillows until they were practically cotton wool and clouds.

The wind howled outside the window and fluttered the curtains as if spectres danced amongst their folds. Martin the teddy bear sat upon the chair beside the bed, keeping an ever watchful eye on the room. The summer heat had broken, but winter's chill was still around the corner.

A single kiss was planted on his forehead, a farewell for the night. His mother's breath felt familiar, reassuring. He winced as if hit with a whip, of course. He had to keep up appearances.

'Sweet dreams, my little soldier,' she said, flashing a wink and a smile as she walked back to the bedroom door. His fingers reached over the top of the covers and gripped them like fat, little worms.

'Night, mum,' he said.

She paused at his door, her own fingers tracing the light switch. Her little boy looked so happy, so healthy. There weren't words to describe the relief she felt. It was like winning the lottery, surviving a lightning strike and becoming a movie star all at once. The rest of the world faded to grey, and all that was colour was Vincent.

'Don't let the bed bugs bite,' she whispered, flicking the light off. She pulled the door to, so that only a knife's width of light cut through the darkness' sudden embrace. She watched him for just a moment before going down the stairs into the living room. It was time to relax in front of the TV with a glass of red.

Vincent rolled over onto his side despite the unrelenting resistance from his bed covers. Through the shimmering curtains he could just about make out the moon, full and bright. Stars hung behind like eyeholes cut in a newspaper.

His clothes were piled up on his chair like the leaning tower of Pisa. His toys barricaded his bookshelf like a miniature army, more stoic than the Queen's guard. His bin was full of empty sweet wrappers. And Martin saw all with his plastic eyes, and didn't judge one bit.

Everything was back to normal.

His eyes closed with the speed of an elderly snail. Soon Vincent was fast asleep.

An hour and a half later his mother retreated to her own bed. She checked in on Vincent, who was motionless. A tiny part of her wanted to rush over and shake him awake, reassure herself that he could, in fact, wake up. But she had to resist the urge. She had to trust that tomorrow would start just like any other day.

She tucked herself into her covers, and the house fell still.

The clock on Vincent's nightstand counted the long, motionless minutes, its hands repeating past the faces of animated mice and dogs. Hushed ticks masked the seconds as they tumbled towards the witching hour.

The light in the hall flickered and buzzed. A whine just on the edge of sound pierced the delicate quiet until it had permeated from background to fore, walking hand in hand with silence. The howling outside the window died down and the curtains fluttered no more.

Vincent's bedroom stood motionless as if trapped inside a glacier. The air was still, sound was denied entry, even the clocks seemed frozen mid-twitch. Only one piece of the picture moved - the gentle rise and fall of Vincent's chest, the trembling of his eyelids.

The closet door slipped open just a fraction, silent in motion. Four fingers, long and black and sharp as the teeth of a rake, caressed their way around the door frame, tapping against the wood like spiders' legs.

The silhouettes of jackets and shirts and cardboard boxes of memories bled into one another to form a towering shape. And from that form came a streak of white, of countless hatchet teeth.

From his room and through the hall there came the sound of laughter.

Thank you for reading Everything Ends. I hope you enjoyed it! If so, why not check out one of my other books…

Everything Ends
Blackwater: Vol. One
Checking Out
Mouth of Midnight
Blackwater: Vol. Two

And if you're interested in some *free* books, I've put together a little bonus for anybody signing up to my mailing list. Just type in your email address and hey presto - free stories. It's completely free and no strings attached - you can unsubscribe at any time. But it's the best way to hear about new releases, discounts, giveaways, and news… so I hope you stay part of the club.

Sign up at my website, and enjoy!

www.twmashford.com

Printed in Great Britain
by Amazon